CAPE BRETON
IS THE THOUGHT-CONTROL
CENTRE OF CANADA

Cape Breton
is the Thought-Control
Centre of Canada

RAY SMITH

BIBLIOASIS
RENDITIONS

BIBLIOASIS RENDITIONS

Library and Archives Canada Cataloguing in Publication

Smith, Ray, 1941-
Cape Breton is the thought-control centre of Canada / Ray Smith.

First published: Toronto : Anansi, 1969.
ISBN 0-9738184-2-5

I. Title.
PS8587.M583C36 2006   C813'.54   C2006-906200-5

Epigraph:
A Small Town in Germany / John le Carré
(William Heinemann Ltd., 1968)

PRINTED AND BOUND IN CANADA

They're about the only ones left who still believe in it all, the Canadians.

John le Carré

Contents

The Age of Innocence

THE STORIES: Youth and hope! How adventurous, how exhilarating, how frightening it was to part the bushes at the edge and begin the journey into the dark jungle of prose fiction. Hacking through recalcitrant undergrowth with an untried machete. Sniffing the ground for possible trails. Tired metaphor: but that's what it seemed to be when I was writing these stories between (as my little notebook reminds me) July 1965 and April 1968. It seemed a lonely exploration.

In one of his many memoirs, Clark Blaise tells of his years of apprenticeship at the University of Iowa: feverish reading of everything in sight, great safaris with new and historical figures, mighty hunters of the word, mighty game from American literature, world literature, even Canadian literature. My jungle was an emptier place; or perhaps I was lazy, or frightened.

Of course I knew something of the great masters, and I understood that as a Canadian I ought to look around for directions from my countrymen. I dutifully worked my way through Morley Callaghan, Hugh Garner, and Stephen Leacock: it was years before I even heard of Margaret Laurence, Sheila Watson or Sinclair Ross. I *had* tried to read *The Mountain and the Valley*: Ernest Buckler was a Nova Scotian like me, but somehow I was never able to get beyond about page five. I recognized that in Henry Kreisel's *The Betrayal* and Douglas LePan's *The Deserter* I was encountering solid writing on big subjects, but I saw no way to use their maps; and I was ignorant in the arrogance of my youth. There was no question that Brian Moore, when he appeared upon the scene, was a writer of superlative, heartbreaking talent. But I sensed I'd never learn my own way from his work; perhaps it was his European sensibility.

The first living, publishing writer I met was Austin Clarke. He burst upon the scene in Toronto like some elemental force; and through Macmillan, when I submitted a first novel (of which more

9

later), I got to meet him. I was pleased, reassured by his generous welcoming embraces: even though I had published nothing, he treated me as if I were one of the gang, another writer. But from Austin's Bajan prose I was obviously not going to learn much about rendering my own impulses. Nor from Mordecai Richler's work: I read *Son of a Smaller Hero, The Apprenticeship of Duddy Kravitz* and *The Incomparable Atuk* with enjoyment, but again without riveting recognition. *Sarah Binks* and *Samuel Marchbanks' Almanack,* however amusing, had the same lack of effect.

Had I been of scholarly or methodical tendency, I would have done a proper search of Canadian literature and perhaps have found something to intrigue me, but in my isolation I preferred to read *The Alexandria Quartet* yet again, to try more Tolstoy, Dostoyevsky, or Chekhov, to get more Hemingway or Fitzgerald under my belt, or to devour the books I most enjoyed reading: mysteries and thrillers. Like an Eric Ambler hero, I walked alone in a cold and possibly hostile world.

But youth is brash. I was twenty-two when I began my first novel; I finished a fair copy fourteen months later. It is set in Toronto where I was living, and there are sections set in Montreal, Ottawa and Muskoka: sort of south, east, north and west, you see. The characters are university students. In an instinctive act of what critics call "distancing," I had the hero come from Vancouver, not Nova Scotia. (His surname, Hood, is stolen from another young writer whom I never expected to meet.) Each of the four parts uses a different one of Eliot's *Four Quartets* as a source of symbol and metaphor; each is governed by one of the four elements. The English Canadian hero falls in love with a French Canadian woman. Among my notes there are diagrams, references to Blake, to the *Anatomy of Criticism,* groupings of character and incident according to opposing poles of static-dynamic, rational-intuitive, chaotic-ordered. The novel is, of course, unpublished.

When I got far enough away from that book, I asked a friend of taste and wit to offer a brief judgement.

"Well," he said, "It proves you have a BA and that you understand the structure of the novel, that you can organize symbols, move your characters about, set scenes, and so forth. It would make a good thesis for an MA in creative writing."

Actually that overrates it.

But I learned a number of valuable lessons. I could actually get something out of my head and onto the paper; I could climb the mountain to a finished book. Those were positive; most of the lessons were negative.

My earnest beavering and the result suggested that if I were bored writing something, it would be boring to read. I saw clearly the error of metaphoric and symbolic schemes imported from outside and imposed upon the material: they would lack conviction; readers would sense the artificiality. I found I had to resist a tendency to set-piece scenes; instead, I should seek more fluid kinds of narrative progression. One note reads: "Stop writing sociological, psychological crap!" I became deeply suspicious of the relevance to me in my work of the standard novel as it developed through the eighteenth, nineteenth, and twentieth centuries: The Great Tradition. Much as I admired and admire Jane Austen, Dickens, Conrad and their colleagues, I suspected they had had all the adventure of inventing and stretching the form, and that a real artist ought to seek forms from within his own imperatives, that forms should arise out of the raw chaos of the material. I found I was bored writing someone else's book.

But theory, even theory arrived at through experience, will not produce art.

While writing that first book, I wrote three short stories for relaxation. They were quirky, fun to write, and suggested certain directions, but they failed in various ways and have never been published.

(The progress of my career is complicated by a second novel which I worked on during various periods over the next three years; I learned various things before abandoning it, but none of the lessons bulks large here.)

My first reasonably successful excursion into the short story was "The Galoshes" (June-September, 1965). It is worked up from several snippets of anecdote from life at Dalhousie University. It is the weakest story in the collection – Black Angus is a pompous failure – but I can still look with a certain satisfaction on some sections for their lightness of touch: the progression of Jasper's encounters with the other tenants is efficient and even enjoyable; I was pleased to have been so successful at what was simply an accurate rendering of a real and surreal apartment building. The conclusion of the two left feet is also anecdotally true, while the composition of the picture of Jasper in Gorsebrook Field was lifted from the Dylan Thomas record jacket with the bird in the snow.

Eight months passed before I tried another short story – "Passion." (May, June and July, 1966; I actually wrote 172 pages during the three months, most of them on the second novel.) All writers succumb at times to the lure of word play. I came out of this story reasonably satisfied that I could play the game too, but with profound gratitude that James Joyce had been called to follow that trail to its magnificent conclusion: my material was elsewhere. Unlikely though it may seem, elements of this story are also based on anecdote: Cathy and Heathcliff are both alive and well and married, but not to each other; a recent photo reveals that she still has long-straight-glistening-goldenhair; so far as I know, neither of them knows the identification, and I think I'll leave them in ignorance.

"Colours" (August-September 1966) eschews wordplay for other aesthetics. My commentary on it in *Sixteen by Twelve* is still in print, so I needn't add much here. The disquisition on the string of pearls I thought a rather obvious explanation of the impulse to particularity, and Dennis Lee was right to place the story first. I was working from the notion that, if nothing else, I should try to get whatever I was writing about so strongly onto the page that its power, colour, spoor would reach up to the reader unforgettably; philosophy, ideas, *the general,* if dealt with at all, should be embodied, not talked through, it should be within the whole story like blood, not worn outside like a T-shirt advertising a tavern. When Van Gogh was doing his sunflowers and Rembrandt his ox carcass they were interested in sunflowers and ox carcasses. My motto was: No Billboards.

My next essay into soi-disant originality was the title story (November 1966-January 1967.) Canadian nationalism was in the air just then, thick in the air in Toronto. Large political enthusiasms (and there were lots about in the late sixties) seem to me to suffer loss of clarity, complexity, subtlety. "Cape Breton . . ." was my attempt to retrieve and fix some nuances in a valid balance. The use of juxtaposition, as mentioned in the story, was certainly not new: I got it from Pound, and he got it from others. This has been the most anthologized of the stories, somewhat through misreading, I suspect. The dream of glorious nationalism expressed through the resistance anecdotes is, for example, undercut in the first sentence of the BC anecdote: "You can't see up through the mist (up through the high timber where the air is clean and good). . ." The parenthesis is meant to be specifically Hemingwayish in tone and vocabulary: the Canadian nationalist, with few home grown dreams, dreams in American terms. I thought the point was hammered home in the last few lines of the story, an exhortation of absurd futility. When Robert Weaver published it in *Tamarack Review* this became my first published story, and I became another in the long line of writers he discovered.

Writing is perforce the loneliest profession, but some painters can chat while working: the sociable profession? My old friend Ken Tolmie was living in Toronto at this time, and I often dropped in to his studio while he was working. Apart from the enjoyment his company always affords, I could watch pictures being made, consider finished works, talk painting. Moving one's mind from one art to another has always fascinated me and I have tried to learn from music and painting; have tried to achieve in words the subtlety of development and the emotional power of music, the visual clarity of painting. Tolmie has often used the camera as a visual notebook, so there were always boxes of photos in his studio. Shuffling through a stack one day, I picked three which interested me, took them home, and tried to write a story around them. The photos were of, as I recall, a graveyard, a gazebo, and a beach. "Peril" (March-April 1967) was my first concerted exploration of indirection. I was also trying to work in a relaxed, even languid progression, unlike the punchy, intense, aggressive (that is, lyric) progressions of "Cape Breton . . ." or "Passion." I was happy with the easy swing of the pieces, but the closures are rather crude, perhaps, almost surprise endings. When John Metcalf selected it for his anthology *The Narrative Voice,* I wrote a commentary which, as is usually the case, oversimplified. But it says a number of things about the way I was working in the story and in the book; it has long been out of print, so I take the liberty of including it here, slightly shortened, slightly altered.

DINOSAUR

1. What I do not write

Walter wanted to stay with her, he did not want to go outside again. Outside you were jostled by people, the eyes of strangers stared at you and hated you for being different from them. Down into the subway, bustle and push, sweat and rush, and up again into the streets to those bloody big doors of Jaspers, VanDamme & Co. "Have you finished the Commissions Post-Due Statement?" And you'd hardly finished your coffee . . .

"Penny for them," said Carol.

He squeezed her small body to him and looked desperately about.

"The light on the ceiling," he replied. "I was wondering what you call that shape. A trapezium?"

"Funny man," and nibbled his ear.

My God, if only she knew, and he squeezed her again, squeezing shut his eyes to keep out the terror and failing.

Who wrote that? When? Where? Obviously part of a novel. Twenti-eth century. English or North American. "Subway" is Toronto. "Penny for them" sounds rather English. Let's leave it for a while.

Call it the bone of a dinosaur and try to reconstruct the rest of the book. It begins the previous Friday afternoon, inside Walter's head. He should be working on Commissions Post-Due but has in-stead been making bad metaphors on the slow passage of time. For a page or two he reflects on past injuries inflicted by the fat pig of a su-pervisor, daydreams of revenge. Miles, another clerk about Walter's age but better looking, a hotshot, owner of sports car, with connec-tions, slips a needle or two into him. Closing time, home for the weekend with Carol. He likes her, thinks he might marry her, but she's a bit dumb and he finds he's coming to hate that one stray strand of hair. . . Rest of novel: Miles gets Carol, Walter makes fool of himself at office party, has several smoothly plotted perceptions about life and people (including another woman), Carol sees too late she was wrong and the novel ends with Walter coming to a larg-ish symbolic, metaphoric and / or psychological perception about life. He acts upon this at about 3:06 A.M. on the dark night of his soul by attacking those bloody big doors at Jaspers, VanDamme & Co. with a blow torch. We are left to guess if he goes insane, gets ar-rested, dies as the doors fall on him, or writes a novel about the spiri-tual agonies of a Commissions Post-Due clerk.

Does your reconstruction look much different from mine? You included a couple of awful parents? Right: the point is, we both have dinosaurs on our hands. If we can reconstruct a novel from a frag-ment it is a dinosaur, extinct, and no damn use to a writer today. It was useful thirty, forty years ago: alive, flexible, adventurous, still growing, still discovering. In a word: healthy.

2. And why

The author? Me, of course. I wrote it an hour ago. It is part of a novel, a large pastiche novel floating around in my head, a novel I hope I never bother to write. Apart from a certain archness in tone which I think is understandable under the circumstances, it seems to me a reasonably convincing bit. It satisfies all the conventions of a standard twentieth century novel. The damnation of it is that I could whip it off in ten minutes. If a writer can do that with a style, with a form, it is dead.

The problem of the artist is to make a representation of the world. That seems general enough to be taken as acceptable by most people. The question immediately following is how to make it.

I deliberately began the last paragraph with "the problem of the *artist.*" Depending on his talents, the artist can make his representation in words, music, painting, dance, whatever. Seen in this light, the hows of the artist extend through a very broad range and my little pastiche fragment is but one of an immense number of hows.

The procedure of my fragment has been widely used for at least a hundred years. Dickens didn't much use it, Tolstoy used it to a degree, so does Norman Mailer. I use aspects of it. But in the twentieth century almost all novels have used it exclusively. Like any other procedure it has its advantages and limitations.

The most important characteristic of the procedure is that it allows a representation of human thought in words. Not symbols (like the big doors), not just figures of speech (having eyes hate), but a sober, prose account of a character's thought. The whole of the book will be contained inside Walter's head, the reader will see the world through his eyes. We find Walter lying in bed, presumably having just made love with Carol. He thinks of going to work tomorrow morning and we follow his mental journey. Certain aspects of the trip are selected so the reader can fill in the feeling of the trip from his own experience. We are told what Carol says, Walter's reactions and words, we see him squeeze her, but we are not told what she is thinking or what is going on somewhere across town, although some novels allow this shift. In addition, we can be sure that no character of importance will appear suddenly more than halfway through the book; that Carol's appearances will be carefully spaced through the story; so also Miles, the supervisor, the landlady. The novel will have a calm rhythm of event, conversation, reflection, action. Walter's problems will gradually mount; they won't fall on him like a load of bricks in the first or the second last chapter. But the defining point is that the book, or the world the book shows us, is filtered through Walter's mind.

The advantage of this approach is that it gives the writer a tool to represent the minds of any number of different people in any number of different situations. (One mind, twenty situations per novel.) The tool can be used in poetry but must be subordinated to the poet's other more important concerns. It can be used in movies, but awkwardly as voice-over narration. It can even be used in painting by lettering the words onto the ground. But it is most at home in prose fiction.

The limitations of the style are several. A lot of thought seems to be in words of a language. But a lot apparently is not. Over a normal day people will have a lot of repetitive thought: "Christ, what a hangover . . . Where did I leave my wallet? . . . I wonder if she loves me . . . Hope it's roast beef for supper . . ." A lot of thought is specific to a profession. Novelists, being novelists, are not accountants or used-car salesmen or farmers in Uzbekistan. They do specialize in imaginatively constructing how other people think and, since young novelists rarely make living expenses from their writing, their biographies often include a line like this: "MacSnurf has been a lumberjack, dishwasher, skip tracer, cabby . . ." Unfortunately, these lists rarely include: "Uzbekistani goatherd, astronaut, banker, senator, ship's captain . . ." Sometimes one of these more recherché types will take up writing as a second profession. If he is good at it, like Joseph Conrad, readers will have something truly unique on their hands. Doctors, lawyers, the odd soldier does this. But very few bankers or Uzbekistani (or Manitoban) farmers. Several generations of writers have tried their hands at creating the thoughts of these people. We have had bankers, bankers with dull wives, interesting wives, mistresses; bankers who hated their jobs, loved their jobs, who didn't care one way or the other; bankers who drank, took drugs, or fondled little girls in parks. A notable feature of such books, though, is that one rarely sees the banker banking. Although

I don't know any books about Uzbekistani farmers, I expect the hero spends a lot of time philosophizing about sky and hills and grasslands; and damned little worrying about diseases of goats or wheat.

This attempt to construct the mentality of various types became a major object of the novel. Books were touted with blurbs like this: "Here is MacSnurf's brilliant and incisive probe into the world of high finance. Through the eyes of Payon Dumand, the dynamic and ruthless director of . . ." This from MacSnurf who, without the aid of an encyclopaedia, would have thought a kited cheque was a native of Prague aloft at the end of a string.

Not only is the imagination limited factually, but it runs out of new people. In his next book, MacSnurf will have to try harder. We have met a thousand Payon Dumands, we want someone with a few extra elements to his character. The end of a process is a hero who is the son of a Bombay brothel keeper and an Arizona cowgirl eight feet tall. Hero was brought up in the north woods of Finland and has had a career as a notary and white slaver in Beirut. Married to a gorgeous but insane Eskimo ballerina [actually married to a brilliant but troubled law student named Sarah: see "Family Lives" in *Lord Nelson Tavern;* this essay was written first] he has retired to Melanesia to catalogue butterflies. The novel relates his train of thought through the ten seconds it takes him to lace up his battered running shoes.

But perhaps the crux of the question lies in the phrase "Through the eyes of . . ." Point of view: once a useful tool, it has become an end in itself, and so a tyranny.

In a sense, of course, there is always point of view. But writers and readers have come to think that a single or at least unified point of view is the norm, the proper form. It is acceptable to get into Walter's mind for a chapter, then into Carol's in the next. But there will be an overall unity of narrative point of view. Anything more extreme and the writer is being deliberately arty, is using artificial contrivance because he can't master the real thing. This is roughly equivalent to insisting that all paintings must obey the rules of perspective, or exhibit the colour theories of the impressionists.

But the only criterion for judging a how is: does it work? A normal beginning for an artist is: "I wonder what would happen if . . ." Right. I wonder what would happen if we said to hell with point of view. Let's try a ten page story with a hundred and twelve points of view. Explode it all over everywhere. Will it work? Yes, I have tried it and so have lots of other artists and it does work. The reader has to be willing to suspend his expectations, but any reader worth a damn should be ready for this from time to time.

Any procedure, then, has its limitations. Until those limits have been reached the procedure is alive. The writer says: "I wonder what would happen if, using this procedure, I tried to represent children . . . love making . . . Marco Polo . . . green men from Mars . . . housewives with very curious hobbies . . . turtles . . ." And he struggles and finds that he can. To reread the book in which some previously untested limit has been tested is continually refreshing. We can go back to Henry James and watch as he explores the limits of point of view. We can read Hemingway or Cary or D.H. Lawrence for their original representations of the world as seen through the eyes of a man with no testicles, a whacky-wonderful painter, or a sensuous English lady. But MacSnurf's novel using point of view as found in *The Ambassadors* and creating a sensuous English lady with the hots for her gamekeeper will be 300 pages of cliché, stereotype, and unintentional parody.

As I said, I'm quite willing to use the procedure of the Walter and Carol passage, but in limited bits, probably for intentional irony, and, I hope, in some new context. But to write entire works that way is to cheat the reader and oneself. The most obvious cheat involves the extensions of the world in the work. The implication of any work is: here is a way of seeing the world. Hemingway says: Life can be seen as a struggle to act with grace under pressure. Lawrence says sex is good. Any book written from a single point of view says the world can be seen this way. But to say: All good novels (or valid novels) show the world from one or a limited few points of view is tyranny and a cheat. [In trying to be concise, I here jumbled together narrative point of view and author's philosophical point of

19

view. But the latter usually requires the former and, as I remarked above, I find political enthusiasms suspect; so I am very suspicious of unified philosophical stances and their extension, unified narrative point of view.]

Another extension and another cheat in the Walter and Carol book is the extension of plot. The statement of any sort of plot is: this is the way of seeing the relations between events; or, this kind of relation between events is a significant kind. Writers have used all sorts of plots. The Greeks accepted *deus ex machina;* we call it a cheat. Dickens and Shakespeare both used lots of coincidence. Their imitators used coincidence as a crutch and a reaction took place. The twentieth-century plot is, in a sense, a massive reaction against plots of shameless junk like the Horatio Alger books. This sort of shift happens when a fresh writer says: "Hold it a minute, it may look fine to you and your readers, but my world is not full of long lost brothers, millionaires in disguise, and runaway horses bearing terrified virgins. In fact, my world hasn't included a coincidence since last Christmas when two of my gift books contained the word "Zeugma". And furthermore, I think it is far more interesting to look at a series of subtle, rather low key events to see if they will lead a character to some significant perception of the world."

Right: and this attitude gave the world fifty to a hundred years of fine prose fiction [Jane Austen to Joseph Conrad, say]. But again, this tool has been used to work just about every sort of material. Its use has become excessive. Writers who use it today without conviction can be seen hiding chance meetings inside pages of elaborate disguise: "How long had it been since Walter had taken a stroll along the river? . . ." So we wade through half a chapter of desultory description of coal barges and used condoms [stolen from *The Waste Land* probably] before we come to: "Dolores, what a surprise to run into you!" "Oh, I often walk along the river . . ." and a few bad metaphors about time passing.

The extension, then, is that there are no coincidences in life. But obviously there are and some of them are damned important and a whole literature which excludes them denies their existence and so misrepresents the world.

3. What I write

"A Cynical Tale" and "Peril" for your pleasure, gentle reader. [I've dropped the few remarks about "A Cynical Tale' from this essay; they are more or less included in the main essay.] In the hope that you see in them, in their extensions, something of the world around you, perhaps even that you see the world in a new and fresh way. A pair of (I hope new) "I-wonder-what-would-happen-ifs." Isn't that what it's all about?

I don't consider them very odd or very new. You should be able to place them, but if you can't, here's a very brief and incomplete context.

They are part of a body of work called "speculative fiction". Generally ironic in tone. Aesthetic in approach; which means, I suppose, an indirect approach to many social and political problems of the world around us. This is in clear contrast to the other rising [in 1971] body of writing which includes things like revolutionary writings, the new journalism, documentary novels and the like, all of which try to grapple directly with the aforesaid social and political problems. I should emphasize, or repeat, that speculative fiction doesn't ignore the world, but approaches it somewhat indirectly. The telling point is that all these types have pretty much rejected the whole creaking apparatus of the Walter-Carol psychological-realism (or whatever it's called) form of writing.

Some big dogs in speculative fiction: Jorge Luis Borges, Vladimir Nabokov. Coming big dog: Kurt Vonnegut, Jr. Prominent younger dogs: Thomas Pynchon, John Barth, Donald Barthelme, Richard Brautigan. Incidentally, from considering these writers, their views, careers, antecedents and whatnot, you can see speculative fiction as a continual historical alternative, trace its ups and downs, off-shoots, roots and other such aspects as critical enquiry can profitably illuminate. [The tradition Leavis might call "Sterne and Other Nasty Triflers"; see the notorious third footnote in *The Great Tradition.]*

Some specific notes on "Peril":

Three incidents which each contain a hidden peril. Three youngish men, rather similar, rather different, take a walk. They meet a stranger or strangers and converse about one thing and another, then go on. In the graveyard walk, the peril is in the necromancer's sanity [along with the slim chance that he may be able to conjure the dead]. (His description of his introduction to the art is, incidentally, a loving parody of Gully Jimson explaining his conversion to painting.) The peril in the park is in the question: Is either of them sane (or is this Chesterton's ghost)? The peril of the beach is that, if everything is as presented (hidden in the geography is the fact that there is only one landward way off the beach and the couple does not have a boat), then Purlieu has lunched with a god and goddess.

I often use "Peril" to illustrate how I write. I began with a cluster of images, moods, words, people that took the shape of a line starting out in front of my eyes toward the right, but curving gracefully to the left and disappearing in the hazy distance. A very relaxing vision. Obviously the curve took shape as the beach in Part 3, but I hadn't thought of the beach when I began to write. [The photograph looked across the beach toward the sea; the curve of the beach was not evident.] It did come out, but the way I consciously tried to produce it in the reader's mind was by arranging and manipulating his expectations. When we read things, it seems to me, we are continually trying to guess what comes next. A long series of correct guesses, as in our reconstruction of the Carol-Walter Dinosaur would be a straight line. An ingenious and convincing thriller like *The Spy Who Came in from the Cold* would produce a jagged line with a jag for every time LeCarré caught us going in the wrong direction. I figured I could make the curve by fooling you just a little every paragraph or so. So if your expectation of outcome had been a straight line running out at thirty degrees on the starboard bow, and if each jolt brought the line a degree or so to port, then the completed line would be a long, gentle curve.

But whether you saw the curve or not (and I don't suppose you did) the story should have left you with a gentle, curving mood. It should have given you some pictures you can't quite explain but which will stay with you for many years, pictures that will return when that sort of mood is upon you or which, returning, bring that mood on. If it did that, then the story worked, and I am happy. If it didn't work for you, then you can use the pages to make paper airplanes to fly in gentle curves and perhaps *that* will make you happy.

4. And why

Because they were there.

That commentary was meant for high school students, which explains in part the rather avuncular tone of some of the remarks. In the light of my college teaching experience since then, I suspect I was writing a mite over their heads, but I was trying to tear down the edifice of 160 years of prose tradition and build a new one in its place.

I left out the part Tolmie's photos had played because it complicated the genesis rather too much. For Ken's next birthday after I finished the story, I made up a large, handsome envelope, and included in it the photos, all the manuscript drafts, a fair copy, and a short commentary.

The Naked Jungle (1954), starring Charlton Heston and Eleanor Parker, is the story of a South American rancher trying to save his estate (and, inevitably, his marriage) from the onslaught of Marabunta army ants which devour everything in their path. The movie played Halifax when I was at Dal, and while I didn't see it until many years later, two of my friends sat in the theatre enthralled. From the movie they developed a school of Marabunta poetry: it also devours everything. The result is meant to be a sort of inspired nonsense, but the inventors quickly realized they had congenial antecedents in the Dada and surrealist movements. Along with a number of others, I had joined in these poetry writing games.

Now (July-November 1967) I wrote the first professional Marabunta short story, "The Dwarf in his Valley Ate Codfish." It is the pearls-not-string theory taken to extremes. The result is an impudent imposition on the average reader, but a sympathetic adventurer can use the detailed intensities of each word, phrase, or sentence to build selections of patterns into a number of valid stories. The main one I read begins with a visit to a hilltop site by two people, one of whom used to live there when it was some sort of estate or school or colony dominated by an older guru figure named The Great Man. The second section deals with crises in the colony, many related to Gladys, one of the members; her affair with the Polish Stanislaus Zeugma results in his running from the colony; he is murdered in a primitive village. In the final section, the colony has broken up, and the members have fled, although a number of them have formed a group (The Shadow People) to make movies.

The story is also an examination of the frustration I was beginning to feel at my continued inability to get anything published; I decided to forge ahead and suffer nobly, trusting that sooner or later I would find sympathetic readers. Both "Colours" and "Cape Breton . . ." had been entered in the *Saturday Night*-Belmont Cigarettes short story contest; neither won, and the second year the judges actually refused to award any prize in the previously-unpublished category for which I was still, regrettably, eligible. I never forgave the judges or the magazine for this sanctimonious refusal to throw a few hundred in tobacco money to some poor unpublished dreamer, whether me or the next wretched scrivener. While I could see that "Cape Breton . . .", the entered story, was weird, surely there was someone else out there writing something suitably traditional for them? They didn't have to publish the winning piece, and some anonymous garret rat would have been ecstatic for six months. I phoned Robert Fulford and made this point to him, but he was quite pompous in reply. I've never forgiven him either.

I have to wonder if I found any sympathetic readers for "The Dwarf . . ." in Alec Lucas's Dell collection, *Great Canadian Short*

24

Stories. In vain I asked him to take any of the others, but I was grateful to him for including me. As it is, his book begins with the Nova Scotian Thomas Chandler Haliburton's "How many Fins has a Cod?" and ends with my codfish piece.

One of the creators of the Marabunta school, Janis Dambergs, later got some Marabunta into print in the bilingual anthology *Babelian Illustrations Babéliennes* (ed. Tristan Max Him, Montreal: *Centre d'étude canadiennes françaises, Université McGill,* 1969). A work not widely available, it is, I can report, much more resolutely incomprehensible than "The Dwarf . . ." Janis appears in "The Dwarf . . ." in the line "J.D. (going under the name of A.C.) once told the crow to go castigate the rood." The crow is quoted from one of his more successful Marabunta poems; A.C. stands for his Marabunta pseudonym – everyone had one – Angelo Cornuto, the cuckolded or horned angel. One of my own lines is printed as well: "No lemon groves o'erhang the hoary Don;" referring to the Russian, not the Toronto river. I don't recall my own pseudonym. Tolmie appears twice in the story: his is the picture in "I see horses . . ." and it still hangs at the top of the stairs in this other house. Ken's are "the feet upon the endless stair" which intrude into the middle of the quotation from Blake of the list of countries. I was typing that paragraph when Ken began walking forward and backward on the stairs up to my study: it seemed too serendipitous to miss. These obscurely private references, inaccessible to any but the closest of friends, do not negate my earlier claim that a stranger with an adventurous mind can retrieve or construct a story pattern of some interest from the work: an archetypal critic should be able to make something of those endless stairs, whether or not Tolmie is walking them. I might add that I heard via the back stair that at about this time a well-known editor recommended me for a Canada Council grant with the argument that, writing as I did, I was never going to make any money. It's perceptions like that that make great editors; he was more accurate than I was then willing to believe.

At times, most writers become interested in what my word processor calls "format" and "font" as a way of manipulating the work on the page. Although the possibilities have tempted me – in the abandoned second novel, for example – the only piece to exploit this sort of surface throughout and which has seen print is "A Cynical Tale" (July, November 1967). Had I known how, I would have ordered up bold face and gothic. The point of surface play is always to dislocate the writer's then the reader's assumptions. Although the procedure is sustainable for two or three pages, I suspect that at novel length it tends to become a distraction for the writer and an irritation for the reader: *Tristram Shandy* is the obvious text to consider. I hasten to add that I early recognized Sterne as one of the great originators of The Alternate Tradition, one in which I was interested in working. I tried the format strategy from time to time – the titles of "Colours," obviously – but only in "A Cynical Tale" have I used it at full length, and have not used it since. The reverse, rather: for twenty years I have insisted on a surface as smooth and transparent as French polished furniture. Let the reader feel comfortable, even complacent with the most immediate experience of the work, the appearance of the page. I go so far as to vary the paragraphing of my fiction so that the reader rarely encounters more than a page or two of solid block paragraphs without an airy break as a rest for the eyes. And further still: the reader must never have to pause to ask who is speaking, where, to whom, or what is happening, since an ostensible why is offered. The excursion into the Barbara Allan story and my conclusions have a good deal to do with this. In my commentary in *The Narrative Voice* I said the story "is about italics, capital letters, parentheses, the semi-colon, a floating point of view, *non sequi-tors,* over-plotting, flat characters, spy thrillers, high rise apartments, lingerie, short stories, overstatement, understatement, dropped endings and plum cordial." This seems to me an accurate sort of description of any good fiction as experienced by the writer writing.

I once turned out for a Montreal Storyteller session expecting to read to a class of mixed grade elevens, and brought nothing with me but the typescript of "A Cynical Tale". Instead of jaded sixteen-year-olds to whom this piece would be only slightly naughty, I found a class of barely pubescent twelve-year-old girls shepherded by nuns. I read with something less than my usual enthusiasm, but was assured later by one of the nuns that her girls were well aware of homosexual yearnings and that the lesbians in the class were accepted with little comment by the others. Reflecting upon that remark, I have to wonder if I deserve the frequent label of "post-modernist."

While my walls are adorned with numbers of drawings by Tolmie and others, I had few colour paintings. In the spring of 1967, I took advantage of Ken's proximity in Toronto to borrow his equipment and advice to produce something myself: I'm a reasonably adroit amateur. First I bought an ornate gilded frame for $15, then searched the library for a picture of the right proportions which might be within my abilities. The result was a serviceable copy of Raphael's *St. George and the Dragon*. I recommend the practice as a means of getting acquainted with a painter. As I struggled with his staggering detail work, I became interested in Raphael, interested and somewhat repelled. "Raphael Anachronic" (November 1967-April 1968) asks the reader to accept a simple enough what-if: what if Raphael could be alive in both the sixteenth and twentieth centuries? (The first two editions have him as *quattrocento*, because he was born in the fifteenth century; but in this edition I have changed it to *cinquecento* when he flourished; his dates are 1483-1520.) The device avoids the distracting mechanical jiggery-pokery of the time machines and time warps of science fiction. It also avoids consistency ("Raphael a Commando" or "Raphael meets Andrew Wyeth") but for a light-hearted and trusting reader, the excursion should provide an amusing introduction to the man.

The conclusion to all these manoeuvrings, deployments and sallies is the final and best story, "Smoke" (also November 1967-April 1968). Here at last I achieved sufficient dislocation for fruitful insight while operating throughout with surfaces and progresses of blithe and beguiling charm. So, at least, it has always seemed to me.

I was trying to produce a story as pungent, as elusive, as evocative as smoke through an autumn wood: the phrase is used quite deliberately in the story. This direction seemed to me, as I began to divine it during the writing of the story, to have been the one I had been seeking: not in character, plot, setting, symbol or any other of the accepted areas was the ground I wanted to map, but in mood and mode. I had seen (as I mention in the section on "Colours") that I wanted to get the spoor of a scene powerfully onto the page, but now I saw that this spoor was both the means and the end of the work I wanted to do. Mood is the feeling I try to work at – happy, sad, amusing, lonely – while mode is the literary type – ironic, tragic, romantic. (This is an oversimplification, of course: the moods and modes are mixed like the voices and parts in a string quartet or perhaps a chamber orchestra.) If a story could be seen as a succession of moods I could concentrate on getting at the soul of a character, an incident, or a section as I wanted them experienced. This sort of thing is very intuitive writing, devilishly difficult to pull off, which is why I take so long between books. The writer must simultaneously go deep within himself, deep into the material, out into the world, forward to possible readers, back in the tradition. He must be self-confident enough to follow the will-o'-the-wisp of hints and humble enough to accept the material's imperatives rather than his own. But the result when it works is fresh and original: humming with the reality of the source material, nothing second-hand. The reader needs only a fairly open battery of receptors to encounter the story not as a crude plot string, an amateurishly rendered psychological confrontation, or an academically approved symbolic pattern (the operating systems in most fiction) but as a succession of moods directly and powerfully experienced. The work then has as its content (in action) the reader's own psyche transmuting through the time the work is being read. The story on the page can be seen as a batch of moods waiting to be released. Scratch-and-smell fiction. User friendly fiction.

This realization as explored in the commentary on "Colours" in *Sixteen by Twelve* and in "Dinosaur" is the basis for my disdain for the overblown claims to originality made by many modern critical theorists: I was there before them and I suspect a good many other fiction writers were too. I also early saw that other writers – Jane Austen or Conrad, for example – could be read as if they were writing as I did; with interesting and fruitful results.

In "Smoke" I first produced both a surface and a progression which satisfied me.

(I also produced what I have been told is the funniest line of dialogue in Canadian fiction: "Shut up and pass me another woodpecker.")

The surface is clean and uncluttered; a reasonably sympathetic reader should find it lies pellucidly on the page: here are no dense thickets of philosophy, no well-trodden and predictable trails of plot, no mazes of psychology, no dark labyrinths of symbol. Here I first comfortably escaped from the leaden tyranny of set scenes as found in, say, "Colours" or "Peril," escaped from the lockstep of commonsensical time in those stories, and without having to resort to the obvious time-play of "Raphael Anachronic" (Milton and Mildred's time machine is an accidental device, not an essential operator.) In "Smoke," for the first time I felt free enough, confident enough to move directly, blithely *as the material suggested, demanded* back and forth in time, hither and yon in space, following the perceived imperatives of mood/mode as they vibrated in the material. Each segment suggested what was to follow; I had only to open myself fully to the thing on the paper in front of my eyes, let it dictate to me, rather than try to control, manipulate, impose upon it.

Let me offer as example a few remarks about a short section, reprinted here for convenience.

Gould and Rachel sat before their fireplace with Paleologue. Paleologue talked in the random way he had about whales and the River Tay. He had read widely. He knew the lives of impresarios and could tell which romantic poets had died of consumption and which of syphilis. Rachel was a dunce with maps, Gould could read them quickly and remember them for future reference, while Paleologue called them tyrannies of the mind and made them seem beautiful. Paleologue walked around things, always around.

("But he can't deal *with* things," Rachel once protested.

("That's of no consequence," replied Gould stiffly. He himself could deal with things, having been trained by his father.

(Milton snickered and went into his back room. He could deal with things better than anyone and his contempt for Gould was as massive as an American car.

("Heh-heh-heh."

(Just what the hell went on in Milton's back room?)

"A mistake," Gould blurted out at last, "It was all a bloody mistake."

"What was?" asked Paleologue, and Gould and Rachel, tumbling over one another, told the story of Ralph and the fly's wings.

"Perhaps it's better this way."

Paleologue was given to musing aloud things which were not entirely clear. He refused to explain himself. He was known to have kept silent about statements which only explained themselves five years later. He was reputed to have made comments which would remain obscure for centuries.

"I suppose you won't explain what you mean," said Rachel.

"Hmmm," replied Paleologue.

THEIR FIREPLACE: Without any fuss or rationalization, we learn that Gould and Rachel have overcome their misgivings in the previous section and have bought the cottage in the woods.

PALEOLOGUE: The name means "ancient words," or "ancient lore." I got it from Robert Graves who gives Count Belisarius in his eponymous novel a tutor named Paleologue; it is also the name of a number of Eastern Roman emperors; and of a French diplomat. My character is a half-half amalgam of Ken Tolmie and a poet friend

30

from university, Michael Kennedy. Paleologue's wife Gussie in *Lord Nelson Tavern* is very loosely inspired by Ken's estimable and beautiful wife Ruth. McClelland and Stewart hated the name Paleologue and wanted it changed, a rare case of a writer winning such a whimsical point. In this segment, I have used anecdotal material about Michael Kennedy.

WHALES AND THE RIVER TAY: A fairly obvious reference to the Great McGonagal's poem on the subject, which Michael had recounted once. Michael was born in St. Andrews, Scotland.

ROMANTIC POETS HAD DIED: A disquisition by Michael in a bar in Edinburgh's Old Town in 1964. I was still trying to get read a few dozen of the basic romantic works; Michael was far ahead of me.

MAPS: I rarely use metaphor, but here the three characters are limned through their relations with one of mankind's great analogues. Rachel is not diminished by her inability to use maps, because she uses a navigational technique called *periplous* by the ancient Greeks; it involves recording the route as experienced horizontally rather than in cartographic overview. Gould (my only published self-portrait) is mechanically capable with maps, but Paleologue is an artist with them. I also rarely use direct comment on characters, but allowed it here as fairly blithe. Michael had once written a poem on landscapes and maps; Tolmie is equally capable of speeches which progress and illuminate like poems.

(BUT . . .): The parentheses are only the most obvious of a number of devices I used for evading time. I was pleased to be able to insert an extra scene so easily; to include without unnecessary machinery a reference to Gould's childhood; and to Milton eavesdropping; and to pose the question.

GOULD BLURTED OUT AT LAST: As conversations will do, this one changes course abruptly. But the change should not be distressing to the reader: it is entirely lifelike. And we can immediately retrieve an evocative picture of Gould fidgeting through the conversation which is lost or masked behind the parentheses. That conversation, we immediately sense, will have been a playful one between Rachel and Paleologue; I'll investigate this a page or so on.

31

TUMBLING OVER ONE ANOTHER: As later Milton and Mildred will go "clambering" and "flailing" through the woods; and later still "scrambling ape-wise toward their destinies." It is the building of such rhythms which makes prose writing such a joy.

PALEOLOGUE WAS GIVEN TO MUSING ALOUD ABOUT THINGS WHICH WERE NOT ENTIRELY CLEAR: As are both Ken and Michael. This is not deliberate obscurity, but an admission of the near impossibility of communication on subjects which require wisdom and art rather than mere knowledge and logic. Paleologue is one solution to the author's knotty problem of writing a character who is smarter than himself.

This was the way to write! Straight to the thing itself, without having to get people out of bed in the mornings, without a recounting of ancestors, without those panoramas of the city which the writer hates to write, the reader hates to read, and TV does better. Without doors which are not doors, stairs which are not stairs, cigars which are not cigars. Without all the clanking machinery of a conventional rendering:

One Saturday in early October, Michael drove over to their new cottage with a bottle of Châteauneuf-du-Pape as a housewarming gift.

"Well it's certainly warm enough today," said Rachel, leading him proudly to the fireplace.

[Half a page of set-up and establishment.]

"McGonagal?" Gould replied. "Wasn't he one of those guys on *The Goon Show?*"

[Subtle: Sellers and Milligan made a movie about McGonagal.]

"No, he was a Scottish versifier of the late nineteenth century. Widely regarded as the worst poet of all time. He wrote on topical subjects. Let me just see if I can recall . . ."

[Quotes from "The Great Whale in the River Tay," or whatever it's called. Good chance for the writer to steal a few laughs without much work.]

"The Tay?" Rachel demanded as she topped up their glasses, [the writer conventionally showing that Rachel is a conventional pre-feminist] "Where and what is the Tay?"

"River and estuary in eastern Scotland," Gould threw over his shoulder. Rachel stuck out her tongue at his blind side. "Issues between Fife and Aberdeenshire at Dundee. Famous bridge disaster." [It was actually between Fife on the south and Perthshire and Angus on the north; we obsessives are left to wonder if the error is Gould's or the author's. Nowadays, with British counties abolished, the Firth of Tay lies between the Fife and Tayside Regions.]

"About which McGonagal also wrote a poem," Michael added with a smile. "An epic."

"Quotations from which are no doubt as exciting as quotations from a map of Scotland," said Gould.

"I wish I knew about maps," Rachel admitted breezily, making it clear that she couldn't have cared less about bad poets, the River Tay, or maps.

"You should learn," remarked Gould. "There's nothing mysterious about them. Useful tools."

"I get where I want to go," she replied.

Michael ran his tongue sensuously along the lip of his glass.

"Maps are metaphors of a most beguiling sort: made by scientists, draughtsmen, as all the best ones are. Beguiling tyrannies of the mind."

Rachel bestowed a kiss on the top of his head.

"Thank you for seeing things my way," she said. "You and I deal with the world in the same way: artistically, intuitively, romantically. Not like some people." She frowned slightly, remembering her complaints about Michael on the way home in the car last Friday night. [Ponderous reminder of potential conflict carefully planted twenty pages ago.]

"Romantics, hell," said Gould firmly. "All romantics die of consumption, which is . . ."

Which is quite enough, for surely the point is made. I don't think my parody is clunkingly crude, is it? And isn't it tantalizingly familiar? How many contemporary novels are written like that? It's about as adventurous, as original, as memorable as a fast food burger, as a sitcom, as a football broadcaster's bogus inflations. ("The Brutes have really come to play football this afternoon, Al!" "Right you are, Earl, but the Thugs may have something to say about that! They've also come to play football, and they're not wearing ballet slippers, I can tell you!" "Which means, folks, we're in for one bruising, bashing, rock-crushing game here today!") With a bit of practice, you can turn out reams of this conventional version "Smoke" progress. Jane Austen pretty much perfected it, she does it far better than I've done in my bit (or most writers have done in their masterworks), and we've had 160 years to learn her lessons and improve on them. Just because this is received technique, it's now dead, so that much contemporary fiction uses progressions so dreary, so spavined, so familiar that we'd be hard put to find anything as tired in a note from Jane Austen to her butcher.

Thus, to my own satisfaction I had at last made a play worth the game. I have to suspect that my new way of seeing my work, my way of writing and reading is not perhaps as obvious to others as I hoped it would be: "Smoke" has only ever been anthologized once, in Ray Fraser's Breakwater collection, *East of Canada*. Nor do I recall any critic ever singling it out as the jewel of the collection. But I had seen my way past my university lessons (so carefully parroted in that first novel) and was writing the real. I enjoyed it so much that, of course, I continued the stories of Paleologue, Gould, and Rachel in *Lord Nelson Tavern*. I wanted to include "Smoke" as a Prelude to the later work, but Anna Porter, who was then with M&S, rejected it because we would appear to be trying to beef up an admittedly slim volume with second-hand goods; and because Milton and Mildred with their time machine were out of tone with the more realistic later episodes and people. Anna was probably right, and as "Smoke" was in print by then I didn't bother arguing the point.

Cape Breton . . . was noticed. There were good reviews in a number of places; I particularly remember Andreas Schroeder's in the Vancouver *Province,* and Sheldon Curry's in what was then the *Port Hawkesbury Sun:* of course, he was one of the few who saw that the "modernist" discontinuities, ironies, parodies and such came indefinably and essentially from Cape Breton itself.

The title caused a certain amount of trouble. For starters, no one ever gets it right, including myself and House of Anansi: if nothing else, the spelling of "centre" is often "center", a peculiar solecism in a book which is allegedly anti-American. It is too long to go easily on order forms, the main reason the book didn't outsell *The National Dream.* It also suggested falsely a regional comedy: ripening codfish under adulterous beds, fiddle music right down on the hardwood floor, Angus and Rory drunk in a dory. Naturally I had given the title to the story. But it was Dennis Lee who was responsible for its being the title of the book. I argued, begged, cajoled, suggested. I lost. The title so embarrassed me that for years I was unable to say it out loud. But I suppose in its own small way it made some noise.

House of Anansi was one of the publishers delivering on the nationalist fervour promised by Centennial year. There really was a Canadian literature and it was here and now. Anansi had primarily published poetry. *Death Goes Better with Coca-Cola,* by Dave Godfrey, one of the press's founders, had been the only previous fiction. *Cape Breton* . . . was the second (designated AF2), and Graeme Gibson's *Five Legs* was the third (AF3), although it was, I think, published simultaneously. Without giving a wholly unnecessary and incomplete literary history of the times, I can certainly say it was exciting then to be a young fiction writer in Canada; genius and daring crashing from the undergrowth on all sides.

Because I didn't read Canadian literature, I was only vaguely aware of the names (except for the other Montreal Storytellers,

Alden Nowlan and Kent Thompson in Fredericton, and Larry Garber in London) until the founding meeting of The Writer's Union of Canada. Such a crowd of congenial people! After a large Union banquet in Toronto's Chinatown, John Metcalf led Alice Munro and myself off to the Colonial Tavern on Yonge Street where Erroll Garner did his casually elegant thing and in the intermissions we chattered away in the warmth of confident friendship. John and I were virtually unknown, and despite a Governor General's medal, Alice was still in the foothills of her long and steady climb to eminence. So we had the intimacy of obscurity and, on my part at least, a queasy, frightening, innocent confidence in the future: I was no longer alone; united we would conquer.

THE COVER PAINTING AND THE DRAWINGS: In my grade eleven classes at Queen Elizabeth High School in Halifax, we were seated alphabetically. So it was that toward the end of the alphabet the order was: Roger Savage, Ray Smith, and Ken Tolmie. In this conjunction, I was lucky in various ways. The other two were painters and I could at least copy, so we set up a company to sell posters during student council and mock parliament elections. The results showed me clearly that if I were to have a career in the arts, it would not be in painting. (I learned in other ways that while I was a competent ham, my career was not to be on the professional stage either.) I had never really taken my painting skills seriously and had from childhood hoped to be a writer. When I looked at the situation with a cold, statistical eye, all our hopes seemed absurd. Three future artists sitting in a row? The odds against are astronomical. (On odds: in the summer of 1968, Anansi sent out a form letter saying it had 120 fiction manuscripts, and they planned to accept one, or perhaps two.) But indeed Ken and Roger are both successful painters, and however my reputation may be judged, I have at least published three books of which I am not at all ashamed.

Among the futures we talked of, I was to write and Ken was to illustrate my first book. When the odds proved beatable after all, I reminded Ken of his promise. He was living in Ottawa at the time

36

and I was in Montreal; as I expected, he accepted the challenge with enthusiasm. I sent him a photocopy of the next to final draft, he did the drawings and shipped them off to Dennis Lee in Toronto. I was mightily choughed: this would be no routine book with nothing but monotonous print.

A week or so later, Dennis called with the bad news: the drawings were terrible, impossible, Anansi could not risk its reputation with such work going out under its imprint. I couldn't believe Ken was capable of anything bad, so the next day I took the Rapido to Toronto and went straight to the Anansi offices.

Ken is so versatile that he can change styles as casually as other people change shirts; I had made the mistake of expecting, of visualizing drawings in a style I'd seen Ken using a year or two earlier; I suppose Dennis had made projections as well. However, while I had to admit the drawings were something of a surprise, I liked most of them at once, and thought some wonderful. But I was in the tenuous position of all writers with a first book in process: how far could I argue before Dennis threw out me and my stories along with the drawings? Not far, it seemed: he was adamant, and only as a favour agreed to allow one, Pierrette with her hat, to appear on the cover. Ruefully I bundled the others together and went to the house of the friend with whom I was staying.

This was another painter, Paul Young. Although he and Ken had met and their relations were cordial, they had never really hit it off, so I didn't expect him to think much of the drawings. Paul opened the package and leafed through them.

"Well," he said after examining half a dozen, "I've always said literary editors were visual idiots, and it's obvious that Dennis Lee is no exception. These drawings are brilliant. My estimation of Tolmie has gone up a thousand percent in the last three minutes."

Music to my ears.

"That good?"

Paul was going through the others.

"Oh yes. Tolmie has brought to the project a wonderful clarity . . . Look at them . . . here . . . and these . . . he has managed an infinitely expansive vision which is also comfortably enclosed. It reminds me of Raoul Dufy."

"If only Dennis could see that."

"Well, of course Dennis should accept them whether he likes them or not. When you ask an artist to do a job, you are approving the result ahead of time. You have to trust that the man knows his business. Which Tolmie clearly does."

But the problem was that I had done the asking. Still, I was immensely relieved, especially because I no longer had to rely on my own shaky judgement. And the more I looked at the pictures, the more I liked them; today, having lived with them for ten years, I love them.

"Do you think there's anything I can do?"

I was thinking of dragging Paul back to Anansi and having him beard Dennis with these arguments of sparkling clarity and ironclad logic.

"From what you've said, I doubt it. If I'd gotten hold of them first I could have had them accepted. When you're dealing with the pictorially illiterate, presentation is all. I'd have made sure they were professionally matted and properly lit when Dennis first saw them, and he would have snapped them up like a dog after a bone. And he would have had a priceless bargain: with these illustrations, this would have been one of the most beautiful books ever published in Canada."

In fairness to Dennis after this exposure, editors and publishers (he was wearing two hats in this transaction) have to trust their own judgements. And I must say that I am very grateful to him for taking the stories, with or without the drawings; he was my first and best editor.

I returned to Montreal with all the drawings except Pierrette. In a gesture of consolation to Ken, I had them photocopied, had Dennis send me two sets of signatures, and so was able to have an illustrated copy of the book bound in morocco for presentation to Ken at the publishing party. I think the price was about $25 at a shop in Old Montreal. I always intended to have a copy for myself, and the other set of signatures still sits on the top shelf of the closet. Somehow, I've never gotten around to it.

After the cover was set up, Dennis mailed Pierrette to Ken, I believe, but Tolmie is so prolific, his studios so overflowing with floods of work that although the unpublished drawings remained together, Pierrette never rejoined them, and has been lost or mislaid. Unless Ken can dig her up, her appearance in this edition will have been worked up from the Anansi cover.

Fortuitously, the painting which brightens the cover of this edition is also by Ken. As the title "Ray and Sandra" suggests, I was the model for the male figure. It is one of several Ken painted at that time using me as model, and was done from photos he took on a day the three of us spent at the beach. Although Sandra and I dated a few times and I was heavily smitten, we were never more than good friends, and so we remain: I last spoke with her four days ago in front of our local supermarket. The scene is the rocky east end of a beach near Halifax which is well known to a number of people who figure in the book: the two who invented the pork chop game in "Colours"; Heathcliff, Mungo, and perhaps Cathy from "Passion"; any number of characters from "The Galoshes"; the two who invented Marabunta; Gould, Rachel and, of course, both the models for Paleologue in "Smoke". Physically, at least, Rachel is in part based on Sandra: they are both tall and statuesque, although Sandra is much more strikingly beautiful than Rachel; in character they have nothing in common. I might add that the beach appears in "The Dwarf . . ." as the seashore where the Shadow People make their movie. It is also the beach in the opening chapter of *Lord Nelson Tavern,* the continuation of "Smoke".

These might all be dismissed as private, sentimental reasons for using this painting. In part they are, but in a large measure they serve to show that this book is suffused with the Nova Scotian sea air which is the essential atmosphere of the work and of my life during those years. Here is the writer gazing at the sea, the woman repeated rather surrealistically and dancing in the waves, here the contrast between the clarity in the rendering and the mystery in the image, here the atmosphere of contemplation and whimsy.

I had never forgotten it over these nearly thirty years, but assumed it had long ago been sold, lost, or destroyed. When Ken mentioned it in one of the telephone chats we had about the drawings, I was delighted to hear it was not just in existence, but accessible for reproduction. I cannot think of a more perfect picture for the cover and I am immensely pleased to see it here.

The drawings, on the other hand, were perfectly accessible: some years after they were so cruelly rejected, I bought them. They hang on walls all over the house, a constant delight and a reminder of what might have been, what, twenty years later, is at last accomplished.

Ray Smith

Secrets from Beyond the Pale

I HAD completely forgotten about the drawings in this book until I got a phone call from Ray asking me if he could use them again. We hadn't seen each other for thirteen years. He said I could write a few comments.

Twenty years ago when these stories were new I was faced with illustrating them. People I knew were in them, including me and my wife Ruth. I didn't always understand them. My ace-in-the-hole was that I had known Ray since high school days in Halifax, and I knew a lot about where his ideas had come from.

All through school and on through university I had listened to his puns. I hate puns and his were loathsome and took much explaining and nudging, but I knew they were a clue to approaching these stories. It may seem unfair to hold his youth up for inspection, but where Ray can tell you about the subtleties of his literary technique and his literary heroes (I particularly remember his love of Pound and John le Carré), I can ask – but where is Pogo, or worse yet, *Mad Magazine?* For *there* is the source – the little trickle that started it all. It did for me, too. Pogo is particularly interesting in that Walt Kelly's use of parentheses and cultural jokes and endless changes of typescript parallel some of Ray's literary techniques years later. The idea of literary playfulness and lateral thinking enters Ray's mind with Pogo.

I used to puzzle over why he makes his characters into literary-cyborgs who seem to rise from the dead of the cutting-room floor. Smoky black and white films in exotic settings could still suck up his language like a parched sponge. Why didn't he make his characters more real? How did language, image, form, and convention become his subject – especially with the voices of the people I knew? In a way he is like a Woody Allen from the Boonies – his subject is culture itself and perhaps its usefulness to him.

Alienation and connection: a two-step you see in James Joyce.

A literature of defeat – you see it also in Ray the Maritimer (a defeated nation) with a Scottish (another defeated nation) Cape Breton (yet another defeated nation) background, using literature as a battle-ground. Ray turns to culture pluralistically, as he does not belong to a singular successful culture that he can believe in or write about. He throws himself and his friends onto its many little stages, and plays them like marionettes. Bravo! The triumph of the imagination turns defeat into escape. His victory is that he has become a writer and he can hear himself think. There is nothing to be said but much to think about, so his art becomes the only possible value in a world whose missions he does not share. What began as teen *angst* long ago evolves into an ongoing portrait of the artist reinventing himself. If your culture cannot sustain you, you must create one to survive. The excesses of nation building of central Canada he simply (and rightly) makes fun of. In fact, given his view of life, making fun of other peoples' cultural cliches is all he can do – this is a literature . . . of total alienation. A literature of deFeets, as Pogo would say. In that, he may be closer to a modern as well as a Canadian spirit than many a more earnest writer.

I think back to Saturday mornings at the Lord Nelson Hotel (the source for the title of his subsequent book) when we, under drinking age, would dress up in sports coat and tie (to dupe the waiter) and order a breakfast of pancakes, sausages, and Guinness Stout. And I look at a painting of Ray and girl at a beach, surrealistically linked by trails of sea kelp, that I painted in 1961. And he is skipping stones on that same beach in a photo, where we often went together, and the skipping stone hitting the surface becomes Ray, seeing how many times he can deflect before he sinks below the waves – and he is us (some of us anyway).

Ken Tolmie

Colours

Colours, colourist, *The Colourist.*
Colour: many app. but n.b. esp. *sb* II 5. "A particle
          of metallic gold." and *vb.* 2. b.
          To misrepresent. *(SOED* – used throughout.)
Indirection.
Episodes, episodic. *vide intra*; II.
The Search.

I. Pillsbury
    sombre, rich; *q.v.*
    London (memory of, not locale.)
    HIS NICHE.

"Port is the well-spring of anecdote, I always say. A few glasses in the
afternoon . . ."

Pillsbury told anecdotes. The first concerned a little girl rather
like Alice who dearly loved her pet civet; the second, almost neat
enough to be fiction, was of a chance meeting with a dwarf on a
train; the third, while amusing, was incomprehensible.

"In those days, though, you could expect that sort of thing . . ."

"Yes."

Pillsbury lived, dwelt in two rooms, alone with his port, his fireplace and his researches. He enjoyed a small fame. On that wet autumn afternoon the shadows stood stacked in the corners like
magazines or memories. On one wall hung a penny farthing bicycle.

"Oh, they're a lot of old fogies." Pillsbury was a fellow of some
Royal Society; it was of the other Fellows that he now spoke. "The
banquets are beastly affairs. Half of them senile and one carries a
whacking great ear-trumpet which keeps getting in the soup."

Pillsbury heaved and pivoted on one elbow to gaze at Gerard,
for his neck would not turn much.

"After all, I'm only seventy-six meself, don't you see?"

Gerard nodded and sipped his port.

"Ahh," sighed Pillsbury, "those were the days . . ."

The landlady brought in a tea-tray. Pillsbury pointed to the low table before him and grunted. She put down the tray and shuffled out again, leaving behind her (or stirring up) an odour of mould which the tea steam did not entirely dissipate.

"I always have my tea," Pillsbury explained, "even out here. There's something to be said for tradition . . ."

Gerard sipped and nibbled and listened for half an hour to what could be said for tradition. "I have a piece in EHR. Can't remember the number but I'm sure the library could dig it up for you . . ."

Teatime and Gerard's visit drew to a close. In desperation he alluded to his purpose in coming.

"Ah yes . . . yes, an enquiry of some sort, didn't you say?"

Gerard had written a letter asking for the interview.

"Well, well. Hum, hem, harmpf . . . I'd like to help, but I'm afraid you've got the wrong man."

"Wrong man?"

"'Fraid so. I've never been to Tibet. I fancy you're thinking of old Philbrick the occultist . . ."

II. Patchouli the Passionate
        gaudy, sordid
        A genre piece: stage, carnival, etc.
        preference of cold cream to Kant.

That night Gerard sat in the dressing room of Patchouli the Passionate at the Club Marrakech and thought about one of the big questions. Gerard disliked thinking about the big questions; he liked particular things, like that jar of cold cream. Surely if one considered a particular jar of cold cream one could . . .

Episodes: that was it, that was how Gerard lived.

Episodes. Take an episode and understand it one way or another. Take It. Belief exists only in action.

45

Episode: interlocutory parts between two choric songs; an incidental narrative or digression in a poem, story, etc., separable from, but arising naturally out of, the main subject; *transf.* Incidental passage in a person's life, in a history, etc.; *Mus.* In ordinary fugues, a certain number of bars allowed to intervene from time to time before the subject is resumed.

Gerard yawned.

Why should the subject be resumed? If the episode arises naturally out of the main subject, then the main subject is . . . in (let us say), is in the episode. Or, say, let us examine the pearls one by one and surely we shall know of the string? Pearls are more interesting than string.

As for the choric songs, Gerard had sat through ten minutes of Patchouli's belly-dancing and there were a lot of people around and Gerard had enjoyed that. After all, one man can't make a crowd scene, rhythmic or otherwise. So, after Patchouli had read Gerard's note and agreed to the interview, Gerard pushed past the chorus (laughter, sweat, smoke, gaping mouths) into the wings and, led by a man with six fingers, came and sat in her dressing room.

Soon the big question (Appearance and Reality or the General and the Particular) drifted from his mind, he yawned and Patchouli came in.

"Hi-ya, Sweetie," she said. "Like the act?"

Gerard explained that while he had only seen a bit of it and was no judge of belly-dancing he had thought it rather good.

"Well, you're wrong; I was lousy. I'm not an exotic at all, I'm a stripper. My agent bungled the bookings."

No, she wouldn't have a cigarette. Instead she ran a glass of water and swallowed a tablet for relief from indigestion.

"It's a rough life," said Patchouli the Passionate.

They talked a while about it being a rough life. Patchouli, her body hidden behind a screen, changed her costume. "I mean, hell, I don't have the costumes to be an exotic."

Gerard noticed that her make-up did not coincide with her features. True, she had two (no more, no less) make-up eyebrows, two make-up lips (upper and lower), two sets of false eyelashes and so on; but while her own upper lip was rather level across the top, the make-up upper lip arched high in the centre and down to points at the corners; and while her own eyebrows, even plucked, curved out and down attractively and naturally, the make-up brows flared up and out at a vicious angle, etc. Gerard's mind was so little interested in the big questions that he quite failed to see the two faces of Patchouli as a metaphor, which failure, had he known of it, would have made him happy.

"I mean, how am I supposed to be exotic in a G-string, you know what I mean?"

He said he thought he did.

Patchouli issued from behind the screen and sat down to replace some sequins on her first G-string.

"Now, this matter I came to see you about . . ."

Patchouli wasn't sure she knew what was the matter, for which reason Gerard had to find a way of referring to her casual prostitution without insulting her.

"Yeah, I seen something of a few colonels in my day. Which one in particular?"

Gerard named one and she said yes she had seen something of him. "But that was two years ago. I haven't seen him for two years. I think he got transferred away somewhere."

Or died, said Gerard to himself. People were always dying.

"What do you remember about him?" He would hide his particular question in a chorus of others.

She said the colonel was something-or-other and Gerard figured out after a time that she meant he was impotent.

"Did he have any scars or tattoos? Any distinguishing features?"

"He had big ears. I suppose you noticed that . . ."

No, he hadn't noticed that the colonel had big ears.

"Well, he had big ears."

Patchouli yawned. Gerard sighed. Patchouli picked at a frayed tassel. Gerard eased into another cigarette.

"Do you remember off-hand if he had long toe-nails?"

"Long toe-nails?"

"Long toe-nails."

"Hummmrn . . ."

The man with six fingers rapped upon the door and told Patchouli she had three minutes. "No rest for the wicked," she sighed. Gerard gave her a wry smile as she double-checked the hooks and snaps of her costume, as she reinforced her make-up. At last he had to cough.

"Oh yeah, you wanted to know if the Colonel had . . ."

"Long . . ."

"Yeah, long toe-nails. Well . . ."

Six-fingers rapped again and called one minute. When Patchouli stood up her joints cracked. She yawned and stretched and walked to the door. Gerard followed with his head down. In the dim hallway they paused. People, noted Gerard, rarely sweep right into the corners.

"Well, I'll tell you, I don't know if he had long toe-nails or not. I'm sorry."

She seemed truly sorry. Gerard tried to reassure her: "Well, ha-ha, at least I know he had big ears."

Patchouli considered this. "You know, I'm not sure now that he *was* the one with the big ears. It's been two years now since . . ."

She had to rush off to her fanfare and her audience. Gerard walked silent, alone in the other direction, yawning.

III.   The Painter

The next morning Gerard climbed two flights of stairs to the studio of a young painter who had a beard. The painter was painting and yelled for Gerard to come in.

"Come in!"

Gerard came in.

The painter stood facing the door with his back to the large windows with the blue north light falling in. Gerard could not see what the painter was painting because the canvas faced away from

48

him. Other canvases and boards stood facing the wall so that Gerard could not see what the painter had painted on them either. The painter stopped painting and offered Gerard a cup of coffee.

"I work pretty steadily," said the painter, "but I always like a break. Only the fanatics can ignore visitors and hunger and such. They're lucky that way. They do so much that some of it has to be good. For the rest of us . . ." – he made a gesture at the turpentine and linseed oil and the tubes of paint – "it's a living."

They talked a while about painting being a living. The conversation consisted of fourteen syllables and lasted some minutes. They both seemed glad they got on so well together.

"Well . . ." said Gerard at last. The painter offered him another cup of coffee and accepted a cigarette in return.

"Do you ever use female models?"

The painter yawned and picked a particle of sleep from the inside corner of his right eye.

"Not much lately. I've been doing landscapes. A few years ago I was doing figures more . . ."

Gerard asked if he remembered a model named Charlene.

"Charlene?"

"That's not her real name; her real name was Virginia but after a while she decided it was inaccurate so . . ."

"Charlene . . ."

"Um."

"But really Virginia?"

"Originally Virginia . . . Yes."

"I'm not sure. Did she have thick ankles? I used a lot of thick-ankled models a few years ago."

"It is possible."

"Um."

With the coffee cup in his hand the painter went around by the window and stared at the painting he had been painting. "Charlene," he said. "Humm." Then, "Look, do you like games?"

Gerard said he liked games (which made the painter happy) so the painter explained a game and Gerard said he'd like to play it.

"It helps me to forget things and then I can usually remember. I play games a lot."

The painter put on a sport coat and they went down the two flights of stairs and to a square near the painter's studio. Around the square were half a dozen bus stops. The painter went and stood in the queue for the 59A bus and after a few people had fallen in behind him, Gerard strolled over. Apparently quite on impulse he stopped beside the painter and shuffled his feet until the painter had finished talking about the weather with a little old lady with a spray of artificial violets on her lapel.

"Uhh . . . say, you don't happen to have a . . . pork chop, I suppose?"

The painter considered this a moment.

"Pork chop? . . . Humm . . ." – he felt in various pockets – "why yes, I believe I . . . yes . . . yes, I do. Here you are."

From the inside pocket of his sport coat the painter took a pork chop wrapped in cellophane. He gave it to Gerard who put it in the inside pocket of his sport coat.

"Thank you," said Gerard.

"'S all right, man. Anytime."

Gerard strolled on to the queue for the 38 and engaged a mother with child in a conversation about the weather. Presently the painter, abstractedly scratching his beard, came . . . "Say, man, do you . . ." etc.

Gerard quickly learned several good lines and tones to use and they played the game three times around the square. Then the painter sat on a park bench and, when his bus had come and gone, Gerard joined him.

"Fine game," he said.

"You play like a pro, really. Better than anyone else I've seen."

"You're not bad yourself."

After a while this conversation died and a while after that Gerard had to cough.

"Uh . . . oh yeah," said the painter, "you wanted to know about this broad named Charlene . . . but really Virginia?"

"Yes."

"Who had thick ankles?"

"Possibly."

"That's right, you did say possibly. You qualified it like that."

"Yes."

"Well, I've remembered."

"Have you? Great."

"Yeah, the game did it all right. Yeah, I can say without fear of contradiction that I have never used a model named Charlene or Virginia or both with possibly thick ankles. I'd swear to that."

"Would you sign a statutory declaration?" Gerard asked cautiously.

"Umm . . . I'm not sure. I mean I'm sure about the broad named Charlene, etc., but I'm not sure I'd sign a statutory declaration, not sure at all . . ."

Gerard wanted to ask for an explanation but he knew the painter would explain. After a minute the painter did explain.

"See, a painter is a few steps ahead of the law because he travels light and fast and the law is big – like an elephant – and goes slowly. This has to be, because the painter is alone and can take chances on unknown ground and narrow trails while the elephant has to be careful or he will trample things under foot and wreak havoc and so on. So painters and the law should avoid each other if possible; they don't get along. It's sad but it's the way it is."

"Yes."

"So when there's a choice, you know, you usually choose . . ."

Gerard waved his hand and said that it was all right, the painter would not have to sign a statutory declaration. They parted on good terms and Gerard promised to come back some day to play the game. He did not come back and he never saw any of the paintings the painter painted. But he did know that the painter would swear at least verbally never to having used a model named Charlene and/or Virginia with or without thick ankles. The painter's memory might have been faulty or the girl might have used a different name. But it was reasonably certain and that was something. It sure made you think.

51

iv. Asp
   a tableau . . . a crack appears
   Pastels: a jungle.
   Focusing

The highest building in the city was topped by a penthouse. The penthouse was decorated with taste. The drawing room of the tastefully decorated penthouse was coloured mauve and white and was softly lit. In this room, in the bay of a window overlooking the city stood a table of great value and on it stood chess pieces of inestimable value. The players sat facing each other on either side of the bay. They would have made a pretty picture for Poussin because of the light, but Poussin was not there; the formalized composition did not allow for more than two people. They were Gerard and an expensive woman of the world called Aspidistra, by friends, Asp.

Asp had been rescued from the gutter at the age of fifteen by an aged, gouty and bumbling ambassador. He was a gentle gentleman. For want of anything better he taught her chess through the long winter evenings. Her game showed promise. Nervously, his hand shaking, his eyes averted, moving, accompanied by unfinished phrases, he gave her, wrapped in decorative paper, several books on the game: Capablanca's *Primer,* Znosko-Borovsky's little book of openings, several by Euwe and *My System* by Nimzovich. She pretended to study them, but in fact slipped out the back way to more interesting games. The ambassador never found her out for her game continued to improve. She possessed a cruel and penetrating tactical sense and never made the same mistake twice.

"Tinkle tinkle," laughed Asp. "Tinkle tinkle rasp." Her 9 . . . N-K5 had opened up numerous variations. Gerard, who had studied the above-mentioned books and others, knew that theoretically the move was unsound. He cast about for its refutation.

"If you were rich, Gerard, I think I could love you."

"I am not rich, Asp. So do not speak of it."

"Glum, glum, Gerard. Tinkle tinkle."

52

The chess set of inestimable value had been sculpted for Asp by a sculptor who had loved her from afar and wished to do so from much closer. It was of ivory with trimmings of gold leaf and had taken two years to complete. He took it to three independent judges who assured him it was of inestimable value (Gerard had checked this) then appeared at Asp's door in the evening (the doorman had seen him enter the building at 7:23: "I was waiting for the duke of J— to take 'is constitutional at 7:25 . . .") with the table of great value and upon it the exquisite box of mahogany open to show each piece resting in its individual velvet-lined place.

"Why, how lovely," Asp claimed to have cried. "Would you like a game?"

"Umm-umm-umm . . ."

People who spend their lives making chess sets of inestimable value do not have time to learn the game. The sculptor suffered so brutal a defeat that Asp laughed, "Rasp," and spurned him.

"He was *so* desolated; it was a shattering experience for him. But then, artists . . ." and right out of the air she made an epigram.

The desolated sculptor took the quickest way out of the tastefully-decorated (olive green and blue at that time) penthouse and other problems (poverty, rotting teeth, etc.): the bay window overlooking the city. In an investigation out of curiosity and not connected with his everyday investigations (like this one with Asp), Gerard had ascertained that the sculptor had hit a borzoi twenty stories directly below (there had been no wind so a few simple trigonometric calculations had proved this) Asp's window at 8:17 on the evening of the day the set had been valued as inestimable by the three independent judges. As to whether or not it had been Asp's window (and not one of those directly below), she did have the set and the table and the sculptor's love for her had been no secret. The world had Asp's word on it (and why should she lie?) that the fall had not been an accident or a murder attempt, but a suicide attempt. The word "attempt" is used here because the sculptor had survived, a featureless blob of gibbering, chess-playing jelly. The borzoi, on the other hand, died instantly.

The refutation of Asp's 9 . . . N-K5 seemed to be in capturing the piece: exchanges are favoured by the positional player who wishes a controlled game which simplifies quietly to one of half a dozen or so basic endgames.

Gerard took the piece.

"Chomp!" cried Asp in delight. "Tinkle rasp."

Nothing disturbed the pastel light. In fact, the reach of a hand to move a piece was illusion; nothing moved for fear of destroying the composition. Sound was light, mauve furniture was light, the white rug was light, the white walls and the mauve walls; the brandy in the brandy glasses but a glint.

Gerard groaned. Leading from the capture of Asp's knight was a line for her which he had judged suicidal. He saw now that it was instead brilliantly sacrificial. Unless Asp blundered, her victory would be undeniable after ten moves or so. He would not resign until she grew bored.

"Gerard, you are a darling, you really are."

"Why so?"

Asp lifted the stopper from the decanter and poured into each glass (or: certain lights altered). Asp detested explanations.

"A . . . friend, a very good friend who is in the army says life is much like war: years of training for a few moments of passionate action."

"That seems possible."

"Have you ever felt passionate, Gerard?"

He had, but said not. She teased him about this a while, answered his moves without ostentation and soon changed the subject to flowers which she also detested.

". . . and daffodils. God!"

"I once ate a daffodil," said Gerard without looking up. "I ate a lot of funny things when I was a kid. I suppose everyone eats funny things when they're kids, even the Queen of Sheba or Columbus or . . . Z— the violinist."

"As a matter of fact, Z— once told me that in his native country at the age of seven he ate an orchestration of Mozart's Symphony No. 40 because . . ."

Because: Gerard was not interested in motives. No. 40 in G minor, к. 550, he said to himself. As soon as decently possible he laid his king upon its side and left.

Asp, fragile light above the chess table, pondered the game a while. Then she began to brood. Some time after that tears filled her eyes and the wonderful pieces of inestimable value upon their table of great value shattered in the tears. She did not know why she was crying. She was crying because the composition was broken and would not anymore have made a pretty picture for Poussin. But then, Poussin preferred outdoor scenes and was long dead.

   v.   Mr. Rufulus
       the crisp and the decaying . . . putrescence . . . horror . . .
       "Ultima Thule" – called by some "the White Island."

The girl at the information desk told Gerard where to find the elevator and what the room number was. He paused at the gift shop and considered a magazine but decided against it. When a man is slipping into death he is not interested in magazines . . . No, that's not necessarily true. He might. Why shouldn't he? But he didn't buy one for he didn't know the man's taste in magazines. On the other hand, perhaps the dying man would just like a magazine, any one at all. By this time Gerard was half a dozen floors above the gift shop and did not bother going back.

The hall was as clean as a new cigarette and for its size contained as much death. The duty nurse pointed out the direction and Gerard walked until he saw the room number. The door was closed and a sign saying "Staff Only" hung from the knob. Gerard considered this a while then took a seat in the little alcove next down the hall.

On a little table beside his chair, Gerard found a pictorial magazine. Because he liked pictures he leafed through it, looking at the pictures but not thinking about them much.

Then he came upon a black and white photograph of a man sitting in a alcove in a hospital reading a magazine. The man's head was bent down so you could not recognize his face. Gerard recognized the hat and the trenchcoat, however. They were his own, or very good copies. On one finger Gerard wore a ring; the man in the picture also wore a ring, though it showed indistinctly due to the modish graininess of the print. Gerard was, it seemed, living inside a rather stale joke. Fortunately he had a rather stale sense of humour.

Here I am looking at myself looking at . . . obviously, myself looking at, etc. That old one. Now, if I look at the camera, will he also look up?

Gerard looked up and saw no camera. Of course, he realized, if I look up I can't see if the picture-man is also looking up.

On the other hand, what if I turn the page? Will he also turn the page? That is, will he continue to do all the things I do or will the page go blank until somebody else sits here to look at it? Is it a picture of me, essentially, or of the alcove?

At last he realized that he need only move an arm or leg and see if the photo-man did it too. The muscles in Gerard's leg had just tensed for the action when he chuckled: no, I shall not do it. This is either miracle or mundane coincidence. If I let it alone, I can always believe it was a miracle.

So he closed the magazine and called to a nurse who had just come out of Mr. Rufulus' room.

"I'd like if I could to see Mr. Rufulus."

The nurse asked, in a friendly enough way, if Gerard was a friend or relative and Gerard explained that he was neither but had made arrangements to see Mr. Rufulus today on a very important matter.

"Well, Mr. Rufulus is very ill . . ."

"Yes," replied Gerard in lower tones. "I understand he will probably not live the night. But if at all possible . . ."

"I'll ask the doctor . . ."

Gerard felt compelled to tell the truth; he had to play by the rules.

"I just wish to ask Mr. Rufulus a question, in person. The answer he gives is of great importance to me, but I must admit it is of no importance to him. If I were allowed it would be a great favour to me. Is Mr. Rufulus conscious?"

"At times. He is very sick."

"Yes."

She went away. Gerard now realized she was quite pretty. He hoped she was also happy.

Some time later a doctor came and, in an English accent, asked the same questions the nurse had, adding the same objections more forcefully. He also picked up the point – which the nurse had missed – that Gerard required to ask the question in person.

"Well, it's difficult to explain. I am making certain enquiries and their validity is – without questioning your integrity, Doctor -called into question when not received directly. Just as you might doubt a patient with a twitching left arm who, in all sincerity, says another doctor told him the twitch was caused by myopia . . ."

The doctor screwed his face into one of those expressions of irony for which the English are so famous. Gerard glanced up, then back at his hands, then coughed.

"Yes, I see," said the doctor with a glance at his watch. "I shall do what I can."

"Thank you, Doctor."

Gerard settled down for a long wait. It would be a near thing. Near things were best. Finding out that a certain newspaper had been published on a certain day was too easy; discovering whether or not a certain native in the Congo had eaten a mango from a certain tree on August the ninth twenty-one years ago was clearly impossible. Mr. Rufulus was going to be a near thing and that made Gerard quiver (as much as he ever did) with the challenge.

At last the doctor returned (while Gerard was yawning) and asked the same questions again. Gerard answered politely and honestly. The doctor put his head in the door of Mr. Rufulus' room and whispered to someone. He nodded to the unseen speaker then to Gerard.

"Thank you, Doctor," Gerard whispered. He was in the presence of death, he could almost feel the soft swish of the blade as it moved in hungry practice.

"Don't thank me. Thank the patient for staying alive."

Gerard considered a pun on patients and patience but decided against it.

A lamp with an intensity control had been turned low. A nurse stood aside to whisper with the doctor. Gerard heard, "Yes, Doctor," and such and understood that he had very little time with Mr. Rufulus. The doctor went out and the nurse closed the door softly. The room smelt of various things.

Holding his hat by the brim, Gerard tiptoed to the bed and sat down. Mr. Rufulus consisted of a thin old face on a pillow. His eyes were closed and his breath came in quick little gasps with long spaces of silence between. Tubes entered orifices.

"Mr. Rufulus?"

All searches are the same. Utter success and utter failure are both perfection and perfection is denied man. The tubes gurgled.

"Mr. Rufulus."

"He is very weak," the nurse whispered. "Even if he can hear you he probably won't be able to answer."

Gerard waited until she had gone to the other side of the room before putting his question.

"Mr. Rufulus, my name is Gerard. I wrote you two days ago because I wanted to ask you a question. Now, I know you are very tired, but I would like very much if you would answer my question if you could. Can you talk at all? Can you say yes or no?"

The eyelids raised a moment and the lips, dry as dry apples, quivered.

"That's all right, Mr. Rufulus, I won't tire you, don't talk if you don't feel like it. Now, I'm going to ask you a question and if the answer is yes, open your right eye; if the answer is no, open your left. If you are undecided, open both, and if you refuse to answer, keep them closed. Do you understand? If you understand, open your right eye, then close it and open your left."

After a few moments the right eye flickered. Then it flickered, then held, then closed. Then the left flickered, held and closed.

"Very good, Mr. Rufulus. Now here is the question: in your

long and honourable life, sir" – the nurse was fiddling with a complex instrument covered with dials and knobs and attached to Mr. Rufulus' orifices' tubes – "did you like parsnips?"

At first, nothing happened.

"The right eye opens for yes, and the left . . ."

The lips began to quiver. They moved up and down with involuntary movement at a great rate like a vibrating guitar string.

"Did you hear me, Mr. Rufulus?" Gerard whispered. He spoke with urgency and his hand went forward as if to clutch the bedclothes or the tubes. The nurse was not watching.

"Mr. Rufulus, can you hear me?"

Mr. Rufulus had apparently heard. His head lifted from the pillow and his eyes opened and turned on Gerard. They opened wide in horror and the toothless mouth opened wide. Still no definite yes or no.

"Just this one thing, Mr. Rufulus. I realize it is of no importance to you but . . ."

Mr. Rufulus' head jerked up another inch and at last the mouth managed a sound:

"ArrhrrhrrH."

Then the head fell back. The eyes stared into space and the horror was still in them.

"Mr. Rufulus! Mr. Rufulus!" cried the nurse.

Gerard got out of the chair and out of her way before she found it necessary to hit him. As she called Mr. Rufulus' name and probed for a pulse, Gerard slipped into the corridor. He would never know now, not directly, at least. It was not the sort of thing a man's correspondence would make clear. The widow might remember Mr. Rufulus liking parsnips but that was of little value. Mr. Rufulus might have been forced during the first month of marriage to say he did and never have had a chance to tell the truth all these years. More serious deceptions exist in every marriage.

The doctor gave Gerard a scowl and ran past. It was too bad. People, searchers all, have no sympathy with the searches of others. The pattern Gerard was seeking might look quite different from the doctor's. But the pattern was there, it was there and it was the truth and all you needed was to look hard enough and long enough and you could find it.

Gerard walked slowly out of the hospital. The sun was due in a few hours and Gerard was tired. He wanted sleep because at noon he was to meet a woman named Culver who might or might not have had a great-grandfather with the middle name of Jonathan. Or was it Nasturtium? Or Bicycle? Ah, well, the details did not matter. In the end there was only the search and, with luck, the pattern. It sure made you think. Gerard yawned.

Cape Breton is the Thought-Control Centre of Canada

A CENTENNIAL PROJECT

Why don't we go away?
Why?
Why not?
Because.
If we went away things would be different.
No. Things would be the same. Change starts inside.
No. Change can start outside.
Possibly.
Then, can we go away?
No. Perhaps. All right. It doesn't matter.

SO YOU BELIEVE in Canada and you're worried about American economic domination? But you can't understand international finance? What you do know is that a landlord can give a tenant thirty days to get out, eh? And the tenant can stay longer if he has a lease, but you don't recall having signed a lease with the Americans?

So you're saying to yourself: "What can I do? What can I do? I can't influence Bay Street . . . what can I do? . . ."

Well . . . uhhh . . . thought of blowing the Peace Bridge?

THE AMERICANS are loath to fight without a divine cause. Assume we provide this by electing an NDP Government, stirring ourselves up with Anti-American slogans like; "Give me liberty or give me death!" or (the most divine of all) passing legislation that is prejudicial to American money.

With their divine cause, the Americans would destroy our Armed Forces in one week. (This makes a fine game; you can play it out on a map.) Canada will have ceased to exist as a free nation.

Now: *Think of the fun you'd have in the Resistance!* It's a great subject for daydreaming: Be the first kid on your block to gun down a Yankee Imperialist.

A VIRGIN named, say, Judy, an attractive girl in her early twenties, is so curious about sexual intercourse that, despite certain misgivings, she goes to a party determined to find a man willing to do the deed. She wears an alluring but tasteful dress, has her hair done, and bescents herself with a flattering perfume.

At the party are certain men of her own age whom Judy knows and finds attractive; and certain men of her own age whom she doesn't know and finds attractive. All realize that Judy is a virgin and that she wishes to experience intercourse. Each feels he would like to help her. At the party are other girls, but they do not figure in the story, being all same as Judy.

The party progresses pleasantly enough. The guests dance and sing and drink enough alcohol to feel light-headed, but not enough to become maudlin, violent, or unconscious. A good time is had by all.

The end of the party nears, and Judy has not yet been offered help. Desperate, she decides to make the proposal herself. In no time at all, the men are seated about her discussing the problem with her. This goes on for several hours until the men pass out and Judy walks home alone. On a dark and lonely street, she is pulled into an alley-way and raped by a stranger who leaves her with her clothes torn, her body sore and bleeding, and her eyes streaming tears.

A week later, her virginity restored in a Venus-wise bath, she goes through the same events. Judy is a happy girl, for she leads a sane, healthy, and well-balanced life.

CONSIDER the Poles. They have built a nation which, if not great and powerful, is at least distinct.

Of course, the Poles have their own language, and they have been around for a thousand years. But they have survived despite the attentions paid them by their neighbours, the Russians and the Germans.

Analogies are never perfect, but the Poles do have what we want. Consider the Poles; consider the price they have paid and paid and paid.

> WIT: Did you hear about the Canadian Pacifist
> who became a Canadian Nationalist?
> SELF: No; why did he do that?
> WIT: Because he wanted to take advantage of the
> economical Red, White, and Blue fares.

RECENTLY a friend conned me into explaining my interest in compiled fiction, an example of which you are now reading.

"Hey, that's great," he said. "That really sounds interesting."

"I'm interested in it," I replied, razoring out the distinction.

"But I hope you aren't expecting to sell any of these compilations. The publishers won't touch anything as new as that."

"Well, that's their business, isn't it? I mean, if they figure it's not for their magazine or it's lousy or something, they reject it. It's a basic condition. If you want to demand they publish your stuff, the best and fastest way is to buy the magazine, fire the editor, and hire a yes-man."

"I didn't mean . . ."

"I know what you meant; but, in fact, the technique isn't new at all. I got it from Ezra Pound and he got it from some French poets. Other precedents might be Francis Bacon's essays, the Book of Proverbs . . . the whole *Bible* . . ."

"But . . ."

My friend babbled on. He talks a lot about writing but, so far as I know, doesn't do any.

YOU CAN'T SEE up through the mist (up through the high timber where the air is clean and good) but you know the dawn is already gleaming on the snow peaks; soon it will reach down here and burn away the mist and then it will be too late. Where the hell is that bloody supply column? You hunch forward between the rock and the tree and peer into the gloom. The armoured-car escort will appear . . . there: when it gets . . . there, Mackie and Joe will heave the cocktails and when the flame breaks Campbell will open up with the Bren . . . Christ, you hope you get some arms out of this because if you don't you'll have to pack it up soon . . . Christ, it's cold, your joints can't take much more of . . . a growl from down around the bend . . . a diesel growl . . .

DO YOU love me?

Yes. I love you. You're my wife.

Why did you say, You're my wife?

Uhh . . .

You said it because you think just because I'm your wife you have to love me when really it has nothing to do with it.

Perhaps. It's more complicated than that.

It's always more complicated. Why can't it be simple? You always say things are too complicated when what you really mean is you don't want to talk to me. Why can't things be simple?

They are. I love you. As simple as that. So simple there's no point talking about it.

Complicated, too, I suppose.

So complicated that to talk about it would always oversimplify it. It's the same with everything.

Then what . . . Oh! You're impossible to talk to.

You know that isn't true.

Yes.

So . . .

Then what is important?

Doing.

Doing what?

Mmmmm . . .

Ohhhh . . .

64

TORONTO is a truly despicable city.

"... like a horse's arse!" Einar finishes. You all laugh because Einar tells a good joke and because you're all damned scared as the car flees through the prairie night. "And what about the girl from ..." Suddenly the night is day ... silence ... then the roar ... Someone gasps, "Did we do that?" You stop the car and stare back down the road at the towering flames ... another flash ... its roar ... and again ... thousands of gallons of oil ... "Well," says Einar, "now I seen the sun risin' in the west. I guess I can die happy." Your laughter shakes some sense back into you: you'd better get the hell out of here or you'll maybe die quick ...

TWO MEN sit on a park bench. They are just men; perhaps office workers enjoying the sunshine during their noon break. For the sake of convenience, let us call them Bill and George. They are acquainted.

    BILL: Nice day.
    GEORGE: Yes it is. Though the weatherman said
             we might get rain later.
    BILL: Yeah, it looks like it.
    GEORGE: It's in the air.

This chatter goes on for a while. Presently Bill remembers a bottle of whiskey in his pocket.

    BILL: Like a sip of rye?
    GEORGE: Ummerrahhohhehh ...

This mumbling goes on until George, quivering through his entire frame, dies.

    BILL: What a crazy guy.

Bill opens the bottle and takes a drink. He sighs with satisfaction, replaces the bottle in his pocket, takes from another pocket a revolver, and blows his brains out.

A DISTANT WHIRR and three more flights of geese knife south through the big Manitoba sky. There was a day when you might have shot at the geese. Now you're waiting for something else to come down the wind through the sedge; there it is, the peculiar aroma of Lucky Strike tobacco and a Texas accent quietly cursing the mud . . .

WELL, I suppose we could move to England.

I hate England, you know I hate England. It rained and rained . . .

Oh hell, it didn't rain that much; that was just overcast and occasional drizzle. Besides we were there in March and April.

Well, it was so dirty. God. I don't mean filth, you know, just . . . grime . . . centuries of grime on everything . . .

But the pubs, don't forget the pubs.

Sure, I know, but who wants to spend every evening drinking beer?

Yeah, I suppose.

Perhaps we could move to the States.

Be serious.

I was only joking.

THE AMERICANS believe they answered all first questions in 1776; since then they've just been hammering out the practical details.

"THEN *boom!*" cries Johnny. "Boom and the plant got no roof anymore, eh? Ha-ha-ha!" The smoky room fills with laughter. Johnny knows no fear . . . but no nothing else either. When will they ever learn? You'll try again; your fist hits the table. "A big boom? Fine. Great. So the papers photograph it for the front page, and it's producing again the next day. But two pounds of plastic at the right place on a few essential machines and this joint won't put out a single ton of steel for two years . . ."

WELL, THEN, consider one Pole. Consider Count Z. Count Z. is a Pole: *ergo,* a Polish patriot. He has his fingers into both the Defence and Foreign Affairs pies. Perhaps he is Prime Minister, perhaps an *eminence grise.* At forty he is vigorous, experienced, and intelligent.

From the window of his office, Count Z. gazes down into the bustling streets of Warsaw. Fifteen years of peace have prompted a cultural revival. In the near distance, several lines of new smoke-stacks puff their evidence of Poland's stable and bullish economy. Count Z. shades his eyes; in the far distance, the wind washes over the wheat fields which, in two months time, should become the third bumper crop in three years.

Yet Count Z. is not happy. Of course he is proud to be leading Poland to a new prosperity. But the peasants on his estate have been whispering an old saying: The Pole only buys new clothes so he'll look respectable when he commits suicide. Count Z. sighs and sits down to his work: how can I commit suicide today? (Count Z. has a subtle and self-deprecating sense of humour.)

An aide enters with the Foreign Office reports. Count Z.'s ambassadors in the Balkans say the Germans and the Russians are supplying arms and money to opposing factions in Bulgaria, Hungary, and Rumania (or whatever they were called in Count Z.'s time). The tension is moderate but unstable. Count Z. frowns.

Next the Count looks through an economic estimate sheet. Trade with Germany will increase by 12.5 per cent over the next year. This is because of a Polish-German trade agreement of two years ago. Count Z. smiles.

But next is the latest note from St. Petersburg. A deadlock has been reached in talks over the disputed ten square miles of Pripet marshland. Resumption of talks is put off indefinitely. Count Z. frowns.

Another aide enters and hands Count Z. a report on Polish defences. He reads it with great interest, although he already knows what it will say: both the eastern and western defence lines are out of date and out of repair. To construct new ones would require half the capital in the country. Financially, given five years, one could be constructed. Diplomatically, however, both must be built at once so as not to risk provoking (or tempting) either the Germans or the Russians. Count Z. sighs. If he were English, he would jerry-build something. But in the holy name of St. Stanislaus, how can he insult his Poland with jerry-building?

67

A visitor is announced: the paunchy, guffawing, monocled Baron Otto von und zu-something-dorf, who was instrumental, from the German end, in working out the trade agreement. After four of his own utterly unfunny and incomprehensible jokes, the German says:

"But my dear Count Z., Poland a Defence Line in the East against the Depredations of the savage Cossack Hordes wishes to build, I understand, *ja?* Your friendly German Cousins – in the spirit which the Trade Agreement possible was made – the Cost of this Defence Line to share would be willing. We Germans, as you well know, *Kultur* love, and we to Civilization a Duty it consider Mankind from the Ravenings of the Bear to protect . . ."

"Sharing only the cost?"

"Well . . . ho-ho-ho . . . of course, we a few Divisions to garrison . . . Transportation Arrangements . . . Security Measures would want . . . ho-ho-ho, and to a Slice of Liverwurst yourself help . . ."

A few minutes after Baron Otto has gone, Prince Igor is announced. Prince Igor is lean and foppish. Only the most delicate efforts prevented his being recalled last year when a prostitute was found beaten to death. He speaks elaborately epigrammatic French, using the occasional Russian phrase to illustrate the quaint wisdom of the peasants.

"Mon cher Count Z., I have heard from Petersburg of the unfortunate breakdown in talks. Of course, love shall always exist between the Tsar and his beloved Slavic cousins . . . The fat Prussian loves war . . . As a token of his esteem, the magnanimous Tsar wishes his gallant Polish brothers to take immediate and indisputable possession into perpetuity of the invaluable ten square miles of Mother Russia. In addition, our mutual father wishes to build for his valiant Polish children a defence line along the Polish-German (ah, that term, it disgusts me: *c'est une mésalliance,* the union of an eagle and a pig) border . . . But will you have a sip of vodka . . . ?"

Prince Igor returns to his villa where he finds his aides taking practise shots at the neighbour's cattle. He tells them of his subtle joke: both the pig and the eagle are interchangeable symbols of Germany and Poland.

This subtlety has not been lost on Count Z. He takes a last look at the bustling streets, the puffing smokestacks, and the waving wheat which may or may not get harvested . . .

In the following weeks, Count Z. more and more frequently plays host to Baron Otto and Prince Igor. As politely as possible, he explains that he prefers Polish sausage to liverwurst; that vodka upsets his digestion. Baron Otto tells jokes which turn like millstones; Prince Igor weaves his *chinoiseries*. They smile till their jaws crack; they drop threatening innuendoes.

Count Z. broods. His wife and his mistress both comment on the pallor of his complexion. He will not be consoled. When he looks into the streets below his office, his eyes imagine a scene filled with arrogant, swaggering Prussians, or cruel, drunken Cossacks. Tension is mounting in the Balkans: a Russian uhlan and a German dragoon have fought a duel in Sofia. The salons are hissing with rumour.

Baron Otto and Prince Igor deliver their ultimata on the same day. Accept the liverwurst and not the vodka, accept the vodka and not the liverwurst, or else. Count Z. takes a last glance out the window and sighs. At least they got the harvest in. He rejects the offers. Three weeks later he is cut down while leading a hopeless cavalry charge.

Some time later, Baron Otto and Prince Igor sit down together in what used to be Count Z.'s office. They agree that the treacherous Poles are a blot on humanity, else why did they start a war they were sure to lose (as has been proven)? Baron Otto and Prince Igor agree to partition Poland, using the line where their armies met as a basis for discussions. There will be no arguments over a few square miles here and there, for Poland is a ravaged wasteland. Of course the harvest will be seized to feed the occupying troops: the Poles are pigs, let them root in the ground for acorns if they are hungry. Prince Igor accepts some liverwurst; Baron Otto praises the vodka.

The Balkan situation is smoothed out. The Germans begin building a defence line along the eastern border of their Polish provinces; the Russians begin building a defence line along the western border of their Polish provinces. These lines will take ten years to build (the Polish slave labourers are so lazy). At that time, both the Germans and the Russians will want to test the other's line. They will go to war. The war will rage back and forth across Poland until . . .

But let the reader construct the rest. Polish history is very simple in this way. The Poles also are simple: they love Poland.

WOULD YOU rather be smothered under a pillow of American greenbacks or cut open on a US Marine's bayonet?

CURFEW for civilians is long past. You sit hunched by the window listening to the laughing soldiers staggering back to their billets. *Tabernacle!* They cannot take a *gros Mol;* it is too strong for them. If you were allowed in the *tavernes* you would show them . . . "*Venez-vous-en les gars,*" whispers Jean-Paul. Silently, silently you slide the window up and wait as the others slip onto the roof. You follow, letting the window slide down behind you. You must hurry; already the others are on the next roof, creeping toward the fourth house along where the CIA is holding Marc prisoner . . .

Visit/ez Expo 67

UHH . . . I guess I'd better tell you I don't like eggs fried in butter.
But . . . but . . .
I'm sorry, but it's true.
But . . . ohh, why the hell didn't you tell me before? God, all this time I've been frying your eggs in butter and . . .
I didn't want to hurt you.
Well, why did you tell me now? Do you want to hurt me now?
No. Of course, you might have decided all by yourself, but if I have any more eggs fried in butter, the cumulative hurt to me (and

70

of course to you) will have been more than the single sharp hurt of telling you. Do you see?

Ohh . . .

It took a long time to decide when was the right moment . . .

Yes . . . yes, I see. Yes. It was the right thing to do.

I love you.

Oh! I love you.

DURING THE winter he was twenty-five, George found his work tending more and more to figure-drawing. He was interested and getting good results. So, as artists will do, he set out to explore the subject more fully, spending most of his time drawing and perhaps three days a month painting this and that in a variety of styles just to keep his hand in. During the next three winters, he got together three shows of the figure-drawings and each year he got better press and sales. *Canadian Art,* as it was then called, gave the third show a very good review indeed.

On the basis of these successes, George applied for and got a Canada Council grant. He used it to visit the Arctic. When he returned to Toronto, he started twelve paintings, forty-three drawings, and twenty-two prints in silk-screen, lino, and wood. He destroyed each upon completion. At last he gave up trying.

For five months he drank, slept with a variety of women, and read detective novels. A newspaper reviewer came to interview him, and George told him to go to hell.

Finally George prepared a canvas, rectangular with proportions of two to one. On this canvas he painted the Maple Leaf flag. He hung this painting on the wall of his studio and went back to drawing nudes. Because he had already satisfied himself, at least temporarily, about figures, the drawings were quite bad. But they got him working again, which is the only way to start. After a few weeks, George found a few curiosities and set about exploring these. They led him back to painting, and since that time his work has gotten steadily better, despite the fact that his recent show received confused and confusing reviews, and one critic was angry about something.

"ARE YOU SURE it's the right cove?' whispers the man in the trenchcoat.

"Keep shut," mutters Willard. Willard is being tough, but it's for the stranger's own good; he wouldn't like going ashore to the wrong reception party. Still, he's got a right to be nervous: it's an hour since you cut the *Rachel B's* engine and no light yet. You peer through the gathering fog. If they don't show in five minutes, you'll have to take the man in the trenchcoat back to the mainland, and that'll mean coming back again and again until you see . . . the light: one long, three short . . . one long, three short. You answer: two long, two short. "Take her in, Willard," and the man in the trenchcoat fumbles with his suitcase while Willard dips the muffled oars into the slick black water . . .

I HAVE HAD stories rejected by a number of magazines in Canada and the US. No American magazine has ever kept a story longer than three weeks, and no Canadian magazine has kept one less than three months.

These stories have averaged ten pages each. That means the Canadian editors were reading just over one page a week; about two words an hour.

Do you realize that most people with the appropriate dictionary can read any language (even limiting it to our own alphabet) faster than two words an hour?

NORTH AMERICA is a large island to the west of the continent of Cape Breton. (Pronounced: Caybrittn.)

SO WHAT if you have to stay at home with the children? Lots of women in France fought in the Resistance; you can do your part too. Take the church supper tonight, for instance. All those National Guardsmen from New Jersey just got homesick; they wanted a home-cooked meal. So Mrs. Parsons said to their commandant, "Why, Colonel, we've always been friendly with your people, living so close to the border. I'm sure the Ladies Auxiliary would love to give your boys a meal . . ." The commandant didn't object when you were chosen to make the soup, and he still doesn't know you've planned a very special soup in memory of your Bill who was shot down in front of his customs shed the day it all began . . .

IF THE Americans would just read their own Constitutional documents instead of memorizing them . . .

DO YOU love me?
>Yes, I love you.
>Ohhh!
>What now, hmmm? Come here.
>Oh.
>What? Eh? What is it?
>The . . . the way you said it . . .
>Said what?
>You know, the way you said I love you.
>What about it?
>You know very well – you didn't mean it.
>I did so . . . really.
No you didn't. You hardly looked at me and you went right back to reading your book.
>I did mean it. You see . . . hell, I hate explaining . . .
(He explains for half an hour. The burden of his thesis is that married love is different from single-people love. Thus, he loves her twenty-four hours a day, loves her in such a way that it affects his whole life, including the way he pours himself a glass of orange juice in the morning. "It is a love beyond saying," he explains. "I state it in my every action, my every word, my every thought. It is like 'presence' or something." He explains that saying "I love you" is for single people and that he prefers not to say it except at certain times when he feels for her that simple, heart-throbbing love of single people that comes to him when he watches her hip as she bends over or as she sweeps her hair from her eyes. "At times like that I say, 'I love you.'" She says she sees and he says, "Do you see?" and she repeats, "Yes, I see.")

I love you.

And I love you . . . I love you.

(The question now is whether he will make love to her or go back to reading his book. The question has no answer because the scene is an amalgam of scenes, one each week since they got married a few years ago. But before they do, one little exchange remains.)

Well then, if you didn't feel like saying, "I love you," why did you say it?

It's better to say it even if it's a technical lie.

What an old funny you are.

Anyway, I love you.

I love you.

SEE, the way I look at it, your problem is that Joe Yank is the biggest kid on the block. Now I know you're pretty friendly with him – him being your cousin and all – but someday he's going to say, "Johnny Canuck, my boot is dirty. Lick it."

Now then, are you going to get down on your hands and knees and lick or are you going to say, "Suck ice, Joe Yank"? Because if you do say, "Suck ice," he's going to kick you in the nuts. And either way, you're going to lick those boots. It just depends on how you want to take it.

Of course, you can always kick him first.

MAYBE we could just stay here.

I suppose.

I mean, I like Canada, really. It's not a bad place.

It *is* home.

Perhaps, though, we could go to Montreal for a change.

Could we?

Why not? Drop your school Parisian accent and unify Canada.

Oh!

We'll have to wait till Expo's over, or we'll never get an apartment; we already have friends there . . . I don't see why not . . .

I love you!
Me too!

THE INTERNAL WALLS of an octagonal room are covered with mirrors. In the room stands a man naked. He is an ordinary looking man; other people would say so if they could get in to see him. They cannot get in to see him because they do not know where the entrance to the room is, or, if they did, how to open it. Likewise the man does not know where the exit is or how to open it. Possibly he would not use it if he could. Likewise back again, possibly those outside would not enter if they could.

In any case, the man is ordinary looking; but at times he thinks himself surpassingly beautiful and at times surpassingly ugly. The man acts out these conflicting feelings, all the while watching himself in the mirrors. With one hand he strokes his beautiful body; with the other (it holds a whip) he lashes his ugly body. The times when he does these things are, it would seem, all times, and they run concurrently.

The situation lends itself to various interpretations. We might consider them; but let us not.

FOR Centennial Year, send President Johnson a gift: an American tourist's ear in a matchbox. Even better, don't bother with the postage.

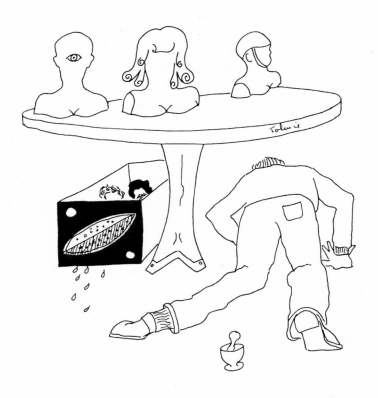

Passion

WATERMELON.

Watermelon!?

Yes, watermelon. You see . . .

How can you argue with a man who replies watermelon? Yes, yes, I, Heathcliff know you must make sibyls of syllables but Sensitivity, Imagination . . . err . . . Feeling etcetera don't count anymore or Cathy would . . .

I don't understand.

You don't unders . . .

Watermelon? No, I . . .

It's you see less; Mungo Rappaport, my oldest and closest friend is, has always been repre appre and incompre hensible.

Well, it's an analogy; I'm folding the case of watermelon against the case of Pleatcliff and Cathy and I think the – he produces a watermelon – analogy is

Perfect. It always is. I still . . .

Ah well, still waters run deep . . . And the watermelon goes back up his sleeve or into a tricky tophat or behind his thumb and I out under the twilight sky banded green and pink like a . . .

Cathy, dreamangel, open your door to waondering . . .

Hi Heatcliff.

With an h please. He-thuh-cliff.

Hi He-thuh-cliff.

Urrrr . . . Polyglot!?

Come dear, it's time for . . .

it. Oh yes, we get along etcetera though out of familyairity I chew a humbug or jujube. In spite it is spicy: anywhereanythyme, urf-urf!? except:

You see, there's this showercap she wears to protect her long-straight-glistening-goldenhair with never a loose strand from my dank and goatish breath and curious hands.

77

Now wasn't that nice, Heatedcliff?

Yes, but couldn't you, I mean, couldn't I just . . .

No, no and no. This fetish of yours is

Annoying, insufferable, atrocious, beyond the pail where we rush (with my foot in it) to the last complete show which she watches while I watch her long-straight-glistening-goldenhair with a swoop sweeping across her forehead . . .

No, Pleasecliff, the way you go on about it is

Insane, incogitable, incompatible, inconciliable, inchoate.

If I marry you will you

No.

Never?

Never.

Not ever?

Oh shh, I want to watch the movie.

Yawns and digital stimulation about the earlobes (taking care not to touch the long-straight-etcetera)

Now, Heavenlycliff, right now, come

Oh you do love me love you do don't you?

Yes love I do love you love

And I love you love

And you do love me love you do

Do, did, done, with that that showercap! against goatishness and when I leave my fingernails fall out but in any case preferably present myself to my oldest and closest friend Mungo Rappaport in the evening of the next day it being hairwashing night which Combthy accomblishes with secret shampooh if you can sham-bear it. Mungo speaks at length about Rhadhe Ateher, a friend who has become the high priest of an apocalyptic English heat cult based in Exeter whilst I mumble expected replies and cogitate upon

Mungo!?

likening the flow of water to the dance of astral fluid

Wig!?

cosmologically sound in the sense that

Mungo! Mungo Rappaport! Listen!

78

to

Mungo wigwigwig!

Waterm

She wears a wig; that's why she won't let me

Nor . . . will . . . she . . . now.

Mungospeech is so concise; point by point, words transfixed two at a time like butterflies on his forking tongue.

Really Fenrock, one fails to

I rush to the night to try not to howl to the haloed moon. Tomorrow (   ) today when small it is over I confront Coolthy with the darning evidents.

A wig? Hogcliff, you're out of your mined. Really . . .

But won't you even tell me yes or

No. Why do you have to be so dogged about it?

I, He-man-cliff (pouncingly): I may be dogged and you my tail but don't you think you can wig-wag me, urf-urf!?

Ohhhhh

But dearsweet, honeybunchy, lovingkindlike . . .

Oh why don't you say things like that to me more often dearest Heathencliff?

Growllll.

After similar titbits I desparit from her arms and home quite desolated (poor blasted Heathcliff) and the next evening drift away to see my oldest and closest friend, Mungo Rappaport who says:

Hello, Centralheatingcliff.

Excretera.

Very funny, but let us get down to brass tacks.

Ow, we cry together, then Mungo in angrage suggests:

Why don't you just strangle the stupid broad if it means so much to you?

I race out of the place bubbling with plans, plots, ploys, schemes, intrigues, sinisters, weirds, etceteras. Exsultan I am, but not to kill her of courts for then what would be the yussef it all, what the pfun? At the drug store I purchase patents, potions, portions, potents with which to do the Catydeed, then awake all night

wildeyed, pointeared, razortoothed, clawfingered, grinning like a
fool, urf-urf, but best of all it is to be administered inside a
Watermelon? For me? Oh! Sweetcliff!
Eatit.
She rushes all over the plates for each of us: Actually no, Catchy,
I've just had a gigantic supper and really, no, I, couldn't, no . . .
Suspicious, nevertheless she gives in and in it goes. Drugged:
Urf-urf, enurf to stop a charging watermelon buffalo.
But she is not buffaloed. Without even raspuking she swallows
it unaffected.
Hendiadys!? I sewear and tongue quietly to myself but am heard
instantly by wide awaif Caffee. Rune! Defeet!
You have lorst, oh! scoundrel, villain, ingreat, speckled viper of
vindows, Oh! Rotten Meatcliff! Little did you know I Cafuly have
studied Zen/Yogurt/Exceter for self control. Go and never darken
mydore again!
Her fair hair: despair! Oh! Gnash! What is the yews? (   ) Small
empty spot here and a bit later with a glass of milk I bite into some
lady's fingers and survey the stock of my new business venture: pem-
mican, chipped beef, jerked beef, jugged hair, etcetera, when my
oldest and closetest friend steps out of the woodwork.
Hi Mungo, take off your
Hatcliff, what have you done?
The draught of sleeping potion did not werk, jerk.
No, for she has been taking instruction from Rhadhe Ateher
himself.
Rhadhe didn't ate her.
You mean . . .
Mean and nasty, yes, I, Eatcliff . . . the remains are packaged
here.
A tradedgy! Horrors! Ghastlys! Terribles! Uncouths!
Actually not bad with whipped cream and a cherry on top . . .
Wastecrag, you are . . .
and maideara.
Doomed.

And the hair was hair. Mungo, Mungo Rappaport, my oldest and closest friend, doome in, slay you will?

Exigencies of the situation, hrumph . . .

They'll never understand the agony of my love. Yes, I mussed fates facts; I could never half got away wif it. Therefore:

Oh! Catherine! Catacombtherine! Catabolthy! Catastrophe! It is I, your Moorwall, I'm combing, I'm combing . . .

A Cynical Tale

SWEET WILLIAM was a very successful fag couturier who lived in a refulgent fag apt. that had cost him five figures. He had a boy-friend named George. Life was very good for Sweet William & indeed he had often been heard to exclaim: "Everything is George!" (one of his loudest clangers). Sweet William was in his thirties.

But then there moved into the apt. next door to Sweet William's an ultrafeminist of undeniable beauty named Barbary Ellen. Barbary Ellen owned a string of health spas, a ritzy speed-reading course for execs. & a language school. Hardly a month had gone by when Babsie had insinuated herself into the good graces of Sweet William. She did this by buying his clothes and sending him cases of plum cordial which was his and George's favourite drink. However, George did not like Barbary Ellen. Barbary Ellen was herself in her thirties & George had made it to his twentieth yr.

One night Swt. Wlm. took George to a cocktail party and what happened was they didn't like it and went home for a plum cordial. *(It should be noted here that Barbary Ellen in fact knew they were going out.)*

When they got home again they found Barbary Ellen had insinuated herself into their apt.

"I thaid she wath a nathty bitch!" This from Grg.

"Goodness gracious!" cried Sweet Wlm.

"Vithious prying creature!" He thereupon scurried off to protect his protector's lingerie.

"Shit." So saying, Babs E. proceeded to pull a neat little auto-matic fromst out her garter holster.

(A NOTE OF EXPL: *All was not what it might have seemed. Sweet William was in fact a Russian spy – having been subverted whilst in Moskva to view the spring collections ("All the sprightly charm of a pre-war tractor") – and Barbary Ellen was in the employ of counterespionage.*)

83

Well!

(Note: *a frail swoon approacheth.*)

Sweet William sank to the Bokhara with a groan & all might have transpired A-Ok had it not been for George who came scampering in at this moment and tried to strangle our lush Barbie Doll with a taupe nylon. Of course she had to shoot him. (THE FATAL FLAW! THE TURN OF THE SCREW! THE LAST TRUMP! *et al.: for B. E. was no less than a latent Lesbian & hated all fags & thus, stupidly, let old George have the full magazine of twelve rounds in the forehead, viz: fitfitfitfitfitfitfitfitfitfitfitfit! The "fit" being caused by the silencer. So.*) Then she put the corpse in the fridge and went on looking for the microfilm which was indeed the very object of her visit.

But! Sweetie W. was not so silly as some of us think fags to be. Not a bit of it! He had craftily secreted about his apt. various and sundry deadly devices of devious but innocent-seeming nature. Thusly, while Barbary Ellen's svelte St. Laurent-suited back *(this being the final insult to Swt. W.)* was turned toward his supposedly swooned bod, Sweet William plucked a sprig of briar from a fag floral arrangement nearby and drove the stem *(previously dipped in a deadly poison by himself)* right the way through Babs' skirt, half-slip & chaste Lycra panty-girdle into her right buttock.

"Fag creep!" screeched Barbary Eln. with somewhat less than her usual aplomb, then lamented as follows: "Me, Barbary Ellen, beaten by a lousy fag creep: Arrgh!"

So saying, she plucked from the same floral arngmt. an equally-poisoned rose clipping and this no-less deadly *fleur* she thrust through S. W.'s shot-silk fag trousers and through his Lycra panty-girdle into his left buttock.

Ah! Irony!

Anyway, they both of them died and their cadavers just stayed there on the floor, one beside t'other. And by some shoddy admin. oversight on the part of their superiors in the spy game, and because the legal eagles conducting their businesses were straight folk thus in love with lucre, the persons of Barbary Ellen and Sweet William *(and of George on ice if it come to that)* were not missed.

And they didn't live in France so there was no concierge to twig & rat.

The briar & the rose, strange though it seems to us of the routine, day-to-day world, took root in the bodies of Sweet Willie and Barbie E. & flowered & intertwined *(symbolic of the love which might have united them in life had not nature played a cruel jest upon their hormonal balances before birth)* & mingled, thus adding a piquant touch to this gruesome tableau, etc.

Peril

I. THE RAIN poured down. It poured down upon the bare trees and the dead grass, upon the bushes and the gravestones. It splashed on the top of the coffin, it drummed on the umbrellas the mourners held, it trickled down Passquick's neck and over his forehead and down the sides of his nose. The rain fell cold out of cold clouds through the grey air: a perfect day for a funeral.

That one, said Passquick to himself, is the widow. Over there is the daughter; those will be friends and relations; that one standing off with the beard and sad eyes, that one is the enemy.

The minister said certain cue words. The mechanism was tripped and the coffin sank slowly into the pit. The minister threw a clod of earth in. The widow shredded flowers. Some of the other men threw clods in. Passquick thought he might do the same, but someone was sure to find he had never known the deceased. They would think him morbid. So Passquick moved away.

Then he noticed, off behind a clump of bushes, the gravediggers. They stood under a tree as if for protection, smoking for the same reason, knowing neither did much good. When the widow goes they will sidle over and cover the coffin. Will they pun together? Perhaps he should circle back and meet them. No, that would not do . . .

At the lane where the cars were parked, Passquick turned and saw the mourners approaching. Near the end of the group was a red-faced man, middle-aged, chubby. That would be an uncle, a travelling salesman of, say, plumbing supplies. "I travel in bathtubs," he would be telling the man beside him. Yes, see, they were chuckling together.

Passquick wandered off through the cemetery, through the rain. Behind him doors slammed and the engines started up. A line of sight through the bushes and gravestones gave him a glimpse of the gravediggers hard at it; they had their work cut out for them.

It was some time later, as he rounded a clump of shrubs, that Passquick ran into the man in the black cape.

"Oh!" cried the man in the cape and leaped up and looked afraid.

Passquick mumbled an apology, bowed slightly (cemeteries bring out the formalities) and turned to go.

"Oh, I'm sorry," said the man. "I thought you were one of the sexton's men. You don't have to . . . It's ruined anyway . . ."

Passquick asked what was ruined.

"The spell, it's ruined now. I'll have to start over again tomorrow . . . Oh, don't apologize; you couldn't help it. Really, it's my . . ."

The man in the cape was middle-aged, thin and bony, the blue veins in his cheeks showing as they do sooner or later on people who use blade razors, and a great beak of a nose. He was dressed all in black, and the black cape hanging to his ankles had a hood which was tied tight around his face and came to a dull point at the crown.

"I'm always frightening away mourners and visitors. That's why the sexton is always after me and that's why I came today, there aren't many people here on rainy days. Most people have the sense to come in out of the . . . oh sorry, of course, you . . ."

Passquick laughed.

"But so are you; so we're senseless together."

The man in the cape didn't take that one at all well. He coughed meaningfully and began secreting his paraphernalia in a black bag.

"What I meant was, if I say we're both senseless and I know I'm not, then you can't be either . . . it was meant ironically . . ."

"Straw for your irony!" said the man with unexpected vehemence. "I've suffered from the irony of the fair-weather friends, of the hail-fellow-well-mets. Cruel, that's what it is, cruel I say, the way you all go on. Why . . ."

"It wasn't meant to be unkind; it was meant in a friendly way . . ."

88

"Yes, I'm sure . . . Well . . ."

They mumbled back and forth until the little man was mollified. Then Passquick asked timidly what the little man did . . . was . . . is . . . err . . .

"Why, I'm a necromancer, of course."

"A necromancer?"

"I conjure the dead."

"Oh yes, of course."

"I'm a journeyman, though I'm not working with a master these days. Journeymen usually work with one master or another."

"It must be hard for you without a master's experience and wisdom to direct and guide your work . . ."

"Well, yes . . ."

The necromancer had all his bones and joss sticks and such in the black bag. As they walked away he explained that you had to be careful, many master necromancers were just frauds.

"Out for a quick buck, shysters, *no faith*. Sometimes you wonder . . ."

As they strolled along he pointed out various graves he had worked: a good job on this one . . . this was the first . . . dropped a brick that night . . . He explained that he no longer worked nights because he was afraid of the dark.

"It's silly, I know, but there are bats and owls twittering and hooting . . . awfully scary . . . and then you occasionally get graverobbers and bodysnatchers . . ."

"That right?"

"Oh yes, and they like to work completely in secret. Don't forget your average bodysnatcher is just a common thug; quite fierce when aroused . . ."

Passquick admitted that necromancy wasn't the simple trade he might have thought it.

"But it isn't a trade!" cried the necromancer.

"Well, of course . . ."

"Trade! How gross! The very idea! Why I'd . . ." That petulance again.

"I mean, I meant it rather as a euphemism. As one minister would speak to another of their 'trade'; it's . . ."

"Then you're a necromancer too?"

There was no doubt about it; as dull-witted necromancers went, this one pretty well took the cake. After Passquick had explained it all and got things going again, the necromancer went on:

"No, you see, necromancy's an art. You must have heard it called 'the art of necromancy' or 'one of the black arts'? Yes, well, that's what it is, you see. Those poets and painters, they like to call themselves artists, but what do they create, eh, what, really?"

"Poems and paintings?"

"Yes, of course, any fool can see that. But what is a poem? Dead scratchings on dead paper. And a painting? Dead paint on a dead canvas. Dead: *no life*. But your necromancer, now, he's a different kettle of fish. Give him dead matter and he puts life into it, real guts, spirit . . ."

Now there was an argument for you; Passquick accepted it as soon as decently possible. The necromancer went on:

"And what does society do? Eh? I'll tell you what society does, it rejects its necromancers. We have to skulk about graveyards, mortuaries and hospitals like . . . like common thugs. We have no artistic freedom; we are scoffed at, humiliated, hunted down . . . you just don't realize what it means to be forced to live outside society . . . most of us are warm human beings who need love, who want to love in return, to be accepted . . ."

"But instead you have to live underground . . ."

Fortunately the necromancer missed it and went on to talk about the younger necromancers he had met.

"Perhaps I'm growing older, perhaps I'm getting a bit conservative, but I think their work is pretty hollow. They've got no style, no elegance, no . . . beauty in their work. Rebels, that's what they are, rebels. And" – he grasped Passquick's sleeve for emphasis – "they don't even know what they're rebelling against, you know what I mean? This new stuff, it's all shallow . . . so shallow . . ."

He shook his head to show the weight of his sorrow.

"Terrible," murmured Passquick. "Terrible . . ."

It was while the necromancer was explaining how he had gone as a clerk with a big brokerage house until one day . . . that he and Passquick came to the gate of the cemetery and found they had to separate, ". . . skinned my eyeballs," the necromancer was saying.

"Well," said Passquick, "it's been a pleasure meeting you."

"No, no, the pleasure was all mine. It's so rarely you meet someone who really appreciates the struggle and the sacrifice . . . The world should make a place for necromancers . . ."

And so they trudged down their separate ways through the cold rain. Amid the cars and the people and the buildings, Passquick felt a great joy in his heart; he floated down the street. When he got home he had a bath and sipped hot lemonade as the steam rose about him. There's nothing like a graveyard on a rainy day, he said, to bring it out in people. But he couldn't think of a word for "it".

2. PERIOD WATCHED the carousel from a distance. Between him and the carousel stretched a green lawn with tree shadows like continents on a map. The lawn was so flat that Period had the impression (as had also many before him) that the lawn could be rolled up on a pole and carried away. (The carpet movers, stout, slow, their cloth caps . . .) The month was May, a morning. The only people about were the women with their children and the pensioners on their benches.

Ump-tiddly music was piped out of the carousel. Period set off across the park toward a bench which was closer to the carousel but off to the right. A course tangential to a point on the radius . . .

But really, he thought, why am I thinking about tangents when I am in the midst of this wonderful scene? Oh joyful! Joyful! The mothers and children and pensioners, he saw as he moved slowly along, were arranged most artfully about. The scene was like a painting in its serenity; yet the figures were too small. It was like music in its harmony; but music was too demanding. Light hung everywhere; the shadows were blinding. The little toddlers toddled roly-poly short distances and their cries and laughs came lightly on the breeze, shattered, the sequence jumbled, random, like a volley of arrows shot by little painted soldiers.

So also the ump-tiddly music from the carousel.

The turf sprang underfoot, green and fresh and young. The melted-frost moisture would still be inches from the surface, nourishing, full of rich goodness, plant food, the cycle of water, interlocking with other cycles, cloud, animal and plant remains, compost, smelling words . . .

Period staggered. He was dizzy, a city man overwhelmed by nature. How can I know, I've never lived on a farm, never grown crops, my lungs dirty from soot and cigarettes, I can't smell the smells true, I can't . . . Nature is also cruel . . . bad years, drought and flood, blight and locusts . . . There's too much . . . I must . . . humility . . .

The park had at least the advantage of being well-treed. Of course, one saw the lamp posts, the gravelled walks, flowerbeds and such, but the trees hid the buildings and streets and deadened the noise enough for a city man to call it almost silence.

But really, such a wonderful scene! And anyway, so what if a park is man-made? Think of it, he thought, as a park, a first-hand park, not second-hand countryside. A farmer would never be able to enjoy a park as much as I can. The birds, for example, are not imported, transplanted country birds, but real live original city park birds.

And the carousel! Four hundred and twenty-three thousand bitter-sweet fantasies about Pierrot and Pierrette. That! for your Colin Clout and other such rude goatherds.

The bench Period had chosen sat beside a path and not far from a fountain (from which he took a drink of chlorinated water – well it wards off the bloody plague, doesn't it?) and gave a pleasant view of the carousel with a blooming lilac bush coyly obscuring it. Period sat down and stretched half a dozen limbs, yawned, groaned, hummed and whistled and finally sat still for at least twenty seconds. Then he enmeshed himself on purpose in the actions of smoking a cigarette – and the earth smells be damned – and decided to think about nothing. It was while he was failing at this that G.K. Chesterton came along and sat down beside him.

"I am G.K. Chesterton," announced G.K. Chesterton.

"Are you really? I'm . . ."

"Of course not. Chesterton has been dead for years."

"That's what I thought. I'm . . ."

"I'm his ghost."

Period couldn't recall what Chesterton had looked like around the face (a beard?), but he knew he had been fat and that he sat in the park a lot.

"Yes, I ghost wrote all his stories, poems and essays."

"Even Father Brown?"

"Especially Father Brown."

"I didn't know Chesterton wrote essays."

"Neither did I. I expect he did though, don't you. If a man wrote stories and poems, he surely must have written essays, don't you think? . . . Or do you?"

"It seems probable."

"Yes . . . that's what I thought."

"Um."

"And who did you almost say you were?"

"Uhh . . . Pierrot"

"That right? You meet the strangest people around a park in the morning. Pierrot, eh?"

"Yes, I live in that carousel over there."

"That's not a carousel. That's a bandstand. A carousel is a merry-go-round. That's a bandstand."

"I know, but it has the same shape as a carousel and 'carousel' has a better sound to it."

"Quite right. Of course. Yes."

G.K. gazed off at the carousel and muttered to himself awhile. Then he undid the neck of his tweed cape and turned to look at Period. There was so much fat about his neck that G.K. had to turn his shoulders too; a very elaborate and dignified movement.

"You're a bit happy for a Pierrot," he said after a time. "I thought Pierrots were supposed to be sad unless there was a Pierrette about. In which case the Pierrot (a) was allowed to be bitter-sweet and (b) would not have the time of day for anyone else. How d'ye explain that?"

"Well, it's true that I've lost my Pierrette, but the fact is, I've been trying to lose her for months."

"That right?"

"Yeah." They nodded at each other for some time. "Not very bright, you know." They nodded some more. "In fact," added Period after a full thirty seconds of nodding, "I would say offhand that when the Pierrettes were lining up outside the brains department my Pierrette was pretty near the end of the line. When she got to the pot . . ."

"Nothing but bone with the marrow sucked out, eh?"

"In other words, yes, a bonehead."

"That was implied in my metaphor," said G.K. stuffily.

"It was also implied in mine; and mine was before yours."

G.K. Chesterton turned enthusiastically.

"Pierrot, I like you. You stand up for yourself. That's the way, meh boy, put 'em in their places; don't be afraid to swagger. Wave the fist. Shake the . . . err . . ."

"Stick?"

"The very word. The . . . very . . . word."

Period nodded and grinned and G.K. Chesterton nodded and grinned. Period stared across the park at the carousel and G.K. stared at him. This went on for a while.

"Tell me though," said G.K. at length, "tell me; your Pierrette, was she pretty at all? I mean . . ."

Period stared.

"Pretty?! Pretty, you ask?"

"Uhh . . . yes, more or less, I guess I did . . ."

Period extended his arms to indicate something which would require great imagination.

"My Pierrette was (is, I suppose you could say), was – is . . . well, even your massive brain cannot (I contend) project an image of a woman possessing half her beauty."

"No shit?"

"Oh yes . . . yes. I tell you, she had a bust . . . well, you wouldn't believe it. Numbers alone couldn't express . . . I mean, I have a certain facility with words, but I'm sorry, I'm afraid I couldn't begin to . . ."

"Don't say you're sorry, meh boy. Sign of weakness."

Period shook his head.

"You're right, of course, Mr. Chesterton. I apologize too much."

"A terrible habit," said Chesterton with terrible sincerity. "A habit which you must . . . *smash!*"

G.K. illustrated this by bringing his fist down with crushing force upon his knee. "Ow!"

"But there's another side to it," said Period, brightening up. "You see, I never mean my apologies."

They went on about this for a while. Then Period went back to gazing at his carousel and G.K. Chesterton took from the folds of his cape a little volume of Hazlitt's essays bound in leather. He began to read one of the essays. Thus they sat for about half an hour.

"Must be off now," said Chesterton at last.

"Going anywhere in particular?"

"Of course not."

"Well, good day. It's been nice meeting you, Mr. Chesterton."

"An honour, I assure you. I might have been Cecil Rhodes and then we'd never have gotten on, I'm sure."

"And I might have been the young Goethe."

"Heaven forbid."

When Chesterton was some distance along the path he turned and called back: "But then meh boy, you aren't such great shakes as a Pierrot."

"No? Why is that? And how would you know anyway?"

"No. Because your feet are too big. And because I say so. Respect your elders and don't be so blasted impudent." He turned and went. The words "young pup" floated back from him inside a balloon as green as your eye.

"It's a carousel," said Period. "And damn the consequences!"

He walked the opposite way along the tangent and not long after that the office workers began to arrive with their sandwiches and their little cartons of milk. Somewhere among them wandered a Pierrette, boneheaded, disconsolate and stacked.

3. PURLIEU CAME OUT of the boulders at the south end of the beach and began walking north. The August sun hung high above his left shoulder and the water lapped and swished on his left. On his right, at the top of the beach, a cliff rose and the cliff was topped with twisted pines.

The day was a weekday so the beach was empty. Purlieu went along doing the various things people do while walking on beaches: he ran, he walked, he picked up driftwood, skipped stones, teased waves, etc. When he had gone a bit of a distance he took off his shoes because sand kept getting in them. Some time later he took off his shirt and undershirt so as to let the sun at his shoulders. Later still he rolled up his pantlegs so as to tease the waves without getting the cuffs wet. Purlieu was doing his usual mediocre job of relaxing.

When he had gone a mile, Purlieu was halfway along the beach. Here the cliff turned away and ran inland as far as the eye could see. Now, at the top of the beach, was a sand ridge as high as a man. This ridge marked a waterline of some sort (high water of storms, perhaps) and was topped with eel-grass. Behind the ridge (Purlieu scrambled up to see) lay a wasteland of sand dunes covered with waving eel-grass. The dunes rolled away for a mile or so until they stopped at the edge of a harbour. The cliff formed the southern edge of the dune waste and of the harbour. The highest of the dunes was in the middle. It rose about twenty feet and had the appearance of a castle keep. Purlieu thought he would like to climb it; he considered this and kept considering it until at last he did not climb it, but slid back down and continued along the beach.

Purlieu had not gone much further when he became aware of the weight of clothing he was carrying. He had his shirt and undershirt, his shoes and socks in his hands. That was obviously pointless,

97

he decided after five minutes' thought; I will put them down on a driftwood log. This he did; and went on toward the north.

The north end of the beach was marked by two man-made structures. Shiny, black, low in the ocean lay the line of a breakwater. The breakwater ran through the surf and on up the beach and in past the ridge at the top of the beach. It kept the beach from sliding into the harbour mouth which flowed just beyond it. Some distance in from the top of the beach (and astride the breakwater) stood a little lighthouse to mark the harbour. On the far side of the harbour mouth rose a high treeless hill with grass of the peculiar grey-green which grass takes on when it has been blasted by gales and kissed by the fog.

It was when Purlieu was halfway along the north half of the beach that he decided to tease the waves again. With his cuffs rolled up and no excess baggage in his arms he became quite daring. So he fell; a wave had teased back.

After much complex deliberation Purlieu came to a decision about his situation: he would take off his wet pants and wet underpants and go for a swim while they dried. The point was that if anyone came onto the beach, Purlieu would have time to get out of the water and into his clothes. Purlieu put the things on a driftwood log and raced into the water.

Well known are the felicitations of a swim in the ocean: Purlieu had a whale of time.

The first thing Purlieu felt when he came out of the water was the immensity about him. The beach swung off to the south in a crescent, one of those sumptuous curves only nature has the patience to bother with. The cliff, which had seemed so high at the time, was a pencil line. Then the sheer waste of dunes, wide as an epoch, and the pretty lighthouse, the hill, the sky and the sea . . .

So, inadequately, the great landscape: Purlieu leaped for joy!

The second thing he felt when he came out of the water was that he was not alone. This for good reason, for he wasn't.

Not far from the pants and undershorts sat an old man in a

wheelchair. Over the man's knees was draped a blanket; in his knobby right hand he held a cane and the cane was stuck in the sand. The old man wore a sleeveless grey pullover over a long-sleeved shirt. On his head he wore a tweed workman's cap. His lower lip jutted out, sunglasses covered his eyes and his head nodded forward and back slightly and continually. The old man did not seem to be looking at Purlieu; he seemed to be looking at the sea. But, of course, the sunglasses . . .

About ten feet to the old man's right and back a bit stood a table. The table was of wood and Purlieu could see that the legs would fold and the top come down and it would thus be portable and like a small suitcase. It had been constructed, Purlieu guessed, in *fin de siècle* England for those elaborate picnics one reads about. Behind the table, preparing an elaborate picnic lunch, stood a young girl, naked.

Of course Purlieu felt certain things upon seeing the naked girl. But she seemed quite unconcerned with her nakedness, with his nakedness, with everything but preparing the lunch. She smiled at Purlieu and gestured did he want any. Of course he gestured yes.

"Wet," said the old man to Purlieu without turning his head to look at him.

"Wet, sir?"

"Yes, sir, wet, sir."

"Yes, sir, I've been in the water."

"The ocean."

"The sea," said the girl and she looked up and smiled.

"How was the water?"

"Fine . . . just right"

The old man's head kept nodding. He did not turn it at all to look at Purlieu and he said nothing else, so Purlieu, rather at a loss for words, turned and looked out to sea. He wished he had a towel to dry himself with. The sun had moved so that it was shining in almost straight across the water at the beach and Purlieu also wished he had sunglasses. He didn't have sunglasses and he didn't have a

towel and he was still too wet to put his clothes on (which he probably wouldn't have done anyway because of the girl being naked), so
he just stood looking out to sea.

"Did you see any eels, jellyfish, or other marine life whilst you
were swimming?"

Purlieu, who hadn't, said he hadn't.

"Perhaps it's the wrong time of year," said the girl.

"Poppycock," said the old man.

Purlieu shifted his feet uncomfortably.

"I used to swim myself," said the old man in a tough voice, as if
he were angry at remembering something he could no longer enjoy.
"I won races at it. We did a different stroke in those days. I think it
was different; I don't suppose we thought much about the type of
stroke we did."

Purlieu went through the elaborate motions of sitting down on
the log beside his clothes.

"Do you race, meh boy?"

"Err . . . no . . . no, I don't . . . race."

"Hunhh."

"Neither do I," added the girl.

And that was that for a while. The old man sat there nodding
and staring at the sea; the girl took from little drawers in the picnic
box sandwiches, radishes, hard-boiled eggs and the like and went on
preparing the lunch; and Purlieu went on in his usual way, looking
and thinking and sooner or later ending up in much the same place
he had started.

At last the girl asked if they would like the lemonade now.

"Why yes, thank you," said Purlieu. "Lemonade would be
lovely just now." The old man grunted a grunt which clearly articu-
lated an affirmative answer. The girl brought them each a glass of
lemonade with ice cubes tinkling.

"Thank you very much," said Purlieu.

The old man grunted ditto.

"The air," Purlieu ventured, "is very bright, isn't it?" It was a
brave venture; he realized this. But it worked out well enough:

100

"Yes," replied the old man. "It is very clean air, clear in a way, yet very full. That is a paradox: clean (or empty) yet full."

"It's the light," said the girl.

"Yes, the light."

At this point the girl began to serve the picnic food. She carried a little tray each to the old man and to Purlieu. The old man's wheelchair had some ingenuity to hold the tray. The girl took a tray for herself and sat on a log on her side of the old man and as far forward as Purlieu so that the three formed an isosceles triangle, broad-based upon the sea.

They all ate with relish.

The little waves lapped and swished against the beach. Purlieu squinted at the blinding sun fragments splashed upon the water. Near to shore the water was a light blue (and light in weight, he remarked to himself) and darker blue farther out. But bright everywhere: the sea! the sea!

During the meal the old man gave a bit of a monologue starting with the smoked oysters the girl had served:

"The molluscs are fascinating creatures and little understood by man," he began. "I have made a particular study of the molluscs and have found out some very interesting things about them . . ."

Purlieu noticed when he next turned to the sea that the sun was now obscured somewhat by high thin clouds which had come out of the west, quite suddenly, as clouds will do upon the ocean. The water darkened and a bit of a breeze sprang up.

"The tide is on the flow," said the old man. "The wind is freshening for the evening."

"It looks like a storm this evening."

"There's gold upon the sea," said the girl.

"No. The storm won't begin till after midnight. But I grant you the sea *looks* like storm in an hour or so."

"Peace," whispered the girl. "Peace."

It was about this time that some combination of the senses suggested to Purlieu that if he looked back over the dunes he would see something that hadn't been there the last time he looked. So he looked.

Apart from a band of light along the ridge at the top of the beach where the light gathered, the tops of the highest dunes with the castle keep off to the south rising high and stolid and the sky above, the dunes seemed much darker than they really were. At first Purlieu could see nothing that had not been there before; but very soon he saw the horseman.

"Why there's a horseman," he said.

"Where . . . oh, there!" said the girl.

"Going to light the light in the lighthouse," said the old man. "Comes from over beyond," and he gestured vaguely to over beyond.

"You can't hear the hooves," said the girl.

"No you can't."

And you couldn't. The sound was perhaps lost bouncing about the dunes. Neither were the horse's hooves visible, for the crest at the top of the beach hid them.

Purlieu and the girl stood and watched the silent horseman ride by. Once or twice he disappeared from view beyond high dunes. For a while he turned as he went to look at them and the light struck his face. After a time he disappeared beyond a dune far off toward the lighthouse and did not reappear on the other side.

Purlieu noticed suddenly that he was cold. But still the girl did not seem to want to get dressed; in fact, she seemed not to have any clothes about. So Purlieu stayed naked.

"Sailors," said the old man, "have a great feeling for lighthouses. Imagine what they feel. It is deep twilight and you are on watch on the starboard bridge wing. There is light in the wheel room but it is low enough to leave you with the dark. Overhead there has been a mackerel sky at sunset and now clouds are gathering in the south-west. It is chilly; the wind is stiffening; you shiver and you think about the rain that will be coming. You look down into the sea which is coursing by: the sea. Here I pause to let you imagine what the sailor feels about the sea."

The old man paused. Purlieu and the girl glanced at one another, then out to sea. Purlieu felt uncomfortable and felt sure the girl did too. He felt certain things about the sea, but as he was not on a ship he felt he probably did not feel as the sailor would have felt.

"And then you look up and there, off the starboard bow, a pinpoint for a moment in the darkness is the light of the lighthouse you've been steering for all week. And now comes a great surge. You remember the peculiar sensation of stepping onto land after a week . . . of the warmth of your favourite waterfront bar . . . of the contrast between the enclosed spaces of land where you can walk for miles and the open spaces of the sea where you live in cramped tension . . . of land and home and love . . ."

For a long time Purlieu and the girl stared at the sea and the sun darkened until at last it slid down into the thin band of clear sky just above the horizon leaving the clouds black and throwing a yellow path over the sea toward them, the yellow deepening to richest gold on the tops of the waves that lapped and swished against the shore.

"The sea . . . the sea . . ." whispered the girl.

"Yes, the sea," grunted the old man.

Then the same feeling came and Purlieu (and this time the girl) turned and saw the horseman riding back between the dunes. In the direct gold light of the sun, the horseman was gold now and he gleamed against the dark sky beyond. When he went briefly behind a dune his disappearances were sudden and surprising; and so his reappearances. And still the horse could not be heard, nor the horse's hooves be seen.

So the three waited; the old man in his wheelchair nodding his head at the sea and Purlieu and the girl, naked, watching the horseman ride by. When the horseman was near the cliff, he turned out of the dunes and continued down the beach to the boulders at the south end. Then the horseman was gone and Purlieu said he thought he would be getting on too.

"It's been a pleasure meeting you," he said.

"And you too, meh boy."

"You don't meet many people on the beach," said the girl.

After other pleasantries. Purlieu began to walk off south. Then he paused and asked if he could help with the picnic box.

"No, thank you," replied the girl. "It's very easy. It all fits together and folds up. There's a place for it on the wheelchair."

"Very cunning appurtenance," added the old man. "Made to give pleasure."

"Well . . ." and Purlieu walked on a way before turning to ask if perhaps they'd like him to wait and walk with them.

"No, that's all right. But thank you," said the girl.

"We go the other way, you see."

"Oh."

He left them like that, the old man staring at the sea and nodding from his wheelchair and the lovely naked girl packing the picnic box. As he walked along he picked up the clothes he had dropped and when he reached the far end of the beach he put them on. It was only then that he turned and looked back.

The light from the lighthouse swung about. It swept the dunes and the beach; it disappeared over the sea, flashed across the hill. But Purlieu could not see the old man and the girl. It did not occur to him until much later to wonder what had been the other way.

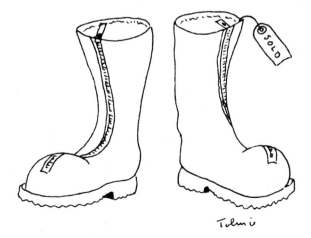

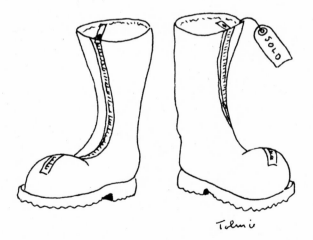

SOLD

The Galoshes

DISMAL IS THE WORD one begins with when talking of February in Halifax. The sun has been known to shine in January or March, but it is under an unrelieved cloak of grey that February sits upon Citadel Hill and broods over that port city beside the sullen North Atlantic. For his first nineteen days, February dwells in the house of Aquarius, the eleventh sign of the zodiac and the deepest pit of zodiacal night. The days remaining to him are spent in the house of Pisces, which stands for the end of all earthly phenomena; Pisces, being a dual sign, has another half, the promise of rebirth, but this predominates only when March has assumed tenancy.

The snow which fell during January brightened the city, but none falls during February in spite of the ominous ceiling of cloud. Rather, January's snow is left to melt during the drizzly grey days and freeze again into large, unsightly crystals in the chill grey nights. Because Halifax is not primarily an industrial city, one does not expect soot, but it comes anyway to impregnate the sterile snow with its sterile seed; the union is celebrated with a solemnity more appropriate to funerals. In the spots where the snow has melted to uncover the husks of grass protruding from the mud, one notices soiled gum-wrappers, burnt matchsticks and the November droppings of furtive mongrel dogs.

Native Haligonians know their city possesses great charm at other times of the year; now they remain inside playing bridge with friends under warm amber light, choosing to ignore February, thinking it only natural, reminding themselves that it could be colder, that spring will be along soon. In homes and offices lights burn throughout the day.

But, for the stranger, companionless, away from home, trying to sleep in a small room on a street at peace with itself, February closes in upon the mind, closing off the world at the rime-encrusted shores of the Harbour, the Northwest Arm and Bedford Basin, blotting out time past at the first of the month and time future at the twenty-eighth. What remains to him is, in the beginning, in the end, and everywhere in between, uniformly dismal.

The winter Jasper spent in Halifax was a leap year. He was attending Dalhousie University and taking courses toward his first year of an MA in English Literature. A Torontonian by birth and upbringing, Jasper was used to crisp winter sunshine. By the fourth day of February he was so close to insanity trying to study that he paced the streets of that forlorn peninsular city in hope of a solitary gleam of amusement, of relief, of light. After three hours he found himself on top of Citadel Hill.

The city lay about him, oblong and featureless. Where a summer visitor saw a rolling sea of lush treetops, Jasper saw only a forbidding stubble which no longer hid the bleak, steep-peaked roofs of the hunched and huddling buildings. Away to the south the North Atlantic churned up whitecaps; on all other sides Jasper saw nothing less desolate. It seemed that all the resources of man and God – if indeed, He had not forsaken the place and flown south with the birds – had been expended to search out all the shades of sienna, umber and grey guaranteed to fill the soul of the viewer with the deepest and blackest depression.

"It is as if," Jasper concluded aloud, "I were standing on the nipple of the one remaining breast of an aged, dismembered and leprous whore."

The metaphor pleased him immensely. In it was concentrated the sum of his experience during the past ghastly week. With everything defined so neatly, Jasper's despondency lessened enough to permit a meagre smile to cross his lips.

"A jar in the nearest alehouse would go down well," he decided, and moved through the slush and the gathering gloom. "Yes, a jar will go down well because it's doing something. Doing something is the secret. Wretches forgotten in dungeons try to stay sane by counting days or studying spiderwebs or weaving blankets from bits of lint. I will fight this thing by doing something."

Yet drinking would not be enough, he knew. February was

everywhere. It got in the nostrils, gave to the eyes a palsied cast, left the hair limp and lustreless, covered the body with grime from head to foot . . . to foot, to foot! Now there was a possibility.

Jasper stopped on a square of dank concrete and looked at his shoes. Once they had been half-decent, comfortable, protective in a fashion; now Jasper saw two pieces of foul, sodden, formless leather. They reminded him of foot-gear worn by serfs in the Dark Ages and described in heart-rending prose in his grade six history book. With the fort on the hill, all he needed to complete the picture was a starved, crazed messenger slogging through the muck gibbering about an impending plague.

But there is something I can do about wet feet; I can buy a pair of galoshes. And that, he decided after counting his money, is just what I'm going to do.

On Spring Garden Road – an incongruous name – Jasper entered a brightly-lit, carpeted shoe shop. Boxes lined the walls, each covered with arcane combinations of letters and numerals which cowed him. For a moment he hesitated, but the vision from Citadel Hill returned and he strode forward resolutely.

"Good afternoon, sir, how are you today?"

"Still breathing," Jasper replied. He liked the unrushed atmosphere of Halifax shops.

"It's warmer today," the clerk smiled.

"Yes."

"Spring will be along soon."

"I'm sure it will," Jasper lied. The clerk indicated a chair and asked if he could be of any assistance.

"I don't suppose you have any galoshes?"

"I just might. They've been going slowly this winter. What size?"

Jasper watched the young man disappear through a doorway at the rear of the shop and heard him whistling as he descended a stairway of seemingly numberless steps. How, Jasper wondered, can he be so bloody cheerful? I expect a Haligonian could laugh in the pit of hell.

"Here we are," beamed the clerk. "Reinforced toe and heel . . ."

Jasper heard no more; he was in a trance. Before his eyes hung an enormous, spineless construction of shiny black rubber. A zipper ran from toe to top and the soles were heavy and pebbled. To Jasper it was a beautiful, yea, even sacred object.

"Right foot please."

"Uhh . . ." Jasper caught sight of the inside and its brown nap lining. So clean, so new it was; soft fibres to keep the feet warm and dry. Did he dare desecrate such beauty with his disgusting shoes?

"They're ten-and-a-halves, you say?"

"Yes."

"Then I won't bother trying them on. Just wrap them and I'll take them with me." When he saw the confusion on the clerk's face, he added charitably, "My feet are so wet now."

The clerk guffawed.

"Won't make any difference, eh? Wet is wet, ha-ha-ha."

"Ha-ha."

With the neat parcel under his arm Jasper crossed the street and walked along to the Lord Nelson Hotel. He moved more quickly now because a chill rain drifted through the darkening street. Rain? In February? He looked at a thermometer on a store front and saw that the mercury stood at thirty-three. A bit colder and we'd have snow; a bit warmer and the rain wouldn't freeze the marrow. But no, February in Halifax offers only the worst of both worlds.

Just inside Jasper sneezed. He sneezed again. And again. By the time he had his handkerchief out he had sneezed six times. Another reason, he thought, for beer. Beer is the best cure for a cold.

The tavern lay warm and almost empty before him; unluckier people had to work. But as he surveyed the room, Jasper saw one face he recognized, the haggard, craggy face of Black Angus Mac-Donald. Black Angus hunched over his beer so that his glistening black hair hid most of his face. He was not a tall man and a grotesque width of shoulder made him appear even shorter. Jasper knew *of* rather than knew Black Angus. A medical student, he had roistered himself a legend on campus so that every student,

111

professor and officer of the administration knew *of* him. As Jasper approached, Angus lifted aside the hair and gave the intruder a dark look. It was a frightening face, the chin cleft deep, the nose straight, the eyes sunk below heavy brows. A scar began at the corner of his mouth and swung in a crescent up to the crown of his high cheek bone. The lightly pock-marked skin would not be, Jasper guessed, unattractive to women.

"Sit down, bye, and have a sip of the malt."

"Thank you, thank you."

"Black Angus MacDonald from the Bay, bye."

"Jasper Johnson. The Bay, you said?"

Pain spread over Angus's face; he stared at Jasper with what appeared to be genuine disbelief until the waiter broke the tension. While paying for two quarts, Angus explained that there was only one "Bay", Glace Bay in Cape Breton Island.

"Where the coal mines are?" Jasper asked hopefully.

"The pits. Ach yes, that's the Bay. And where are you from that you haven't heard o' the Bay?"

"Toronto."

"A Dhia, is that a fact now? Would you be after knowing me uncle, Red Rory MacDonald the carpenter? He lives in Hamilton. That's not far from Toronto, is it now?"

"About forty miles. No, I'm afraid I don't know your uncle."

Angus drained his glass and poured another, all the time holding Jasper in a cancerous gaze. "Ach, but that's a damn shame indeed. How about Sander Beaton? Or Dan Hector Ferry-me-over?"

"Afraid not."

"What about Dougald Joe Gillis, known as The Lobster? Works on the Toronto Subway. Ye don't know him either? What the hell's the good o' ye then? Eh?"

Jasper cleaned his glasses with great care and explained he studied hard in Toronto and met few people. It was the best lie he could manufacture.

"Ah well, I suppose Toronto is a big city, too. At least twice or three times as big as the Bay. You wouldn't get to meet everyone, would you?"

A suspicious note in the voice made Jasper sneak a glance. The eyes were no longer glazed, but sparkled with great good humour. Jasper, the city slicker, had been taken.

"But you never can tell," he essayed. "Cape Bretoners are well known in Toronto. I might meet one when I go back."

"That's true," Angus replied in unaccented English. "Try the NES on Adelaide Street; the Bay byes are there every week to collect their pogey when construction work is slow. But did you know that the late Sidney Smith, once president of U of T and later Minister of External Affairs was a Cape Bretoner?"

"Yes," Jasper lied again.

"D'ye know yer lyin'? Right down close to the hardwood floor, bye. But tell me, can ye do a step or two?"

"A step?"

"A step, a dance? Don't they teach you anything in the big city?"

Jasper rubbed his chin pensively and drew from his overcoat an alto recorder. Angus let out a whoop as the music trickled about the tavern. Dancing and playing, the party was moving well when Jasper tried to stop.

"More, more, a bit of a jig if ye can. And put some bloody guts into it this time."

Jasper piped a lively tune written by Henry VIII. The Cape Bretoner metamorphosed into a rollicking step the music written centuries before by the Tudor monarch. It seemed to Jasper that the two would have gotten on famously together.

"All right boys, I'm sorry, but you'll have to break it up."

Angus stopped dead and glared at the waiter like a great stupid bull. The glaze filmed his eyes and the waiter swabbed the table to avoid them.

"Ach, who ever said Halifax was anything but a barbarous town anyway?"

"Now look Angus, the law is the same here as in the Bay. If the inspector comes in we lose our licence."

"And a damn good thing it would be. But I'll not drink in a

heathenish, stinking pigsty. I'll have the Health Department down on you, no Goddamn fierce I won't. Hitch up your harse, Jasper, we'll move to more congenial premises."

As they stepped into the dark street with the light glistening through the rain, Angus said, *"Angst,* that's German for Angus, isn't it?"

"I thought it was for anxiety."

"What the hell you think Angus is Gaelic for? You must be a bloody artsman."

"English MA."

"Frustrated writer."

"No. Honest to God aesthetician."

"Bloody damn good. The best philosopher since Aristotle would be an aesthetician with guts. Just imagine combining philosophy and guts. What would you be if you could? Eh?"

More Angus anecdotes came back to Jasper. One was that Angus held the record for passing exams while drunk. And consistently led his class. Then there was the philosophy course Angus audited. He behaved well in class all winter and attended every lecture in a sober state. One week before exams he paid the extra fees to become a regular student; he received the only first.

"If you combined aesthetics and guts, you'd be . . . I don't know . . . Shakespeare the butcher?"

Angus held open the restaurant door and Jasper stepped into the warm, dim interior. The hostess, looking cool and un-Haligonian in a slim black dress was just approaching when Angus answered in a voice of perfectly controlled volume: "You'd be bloody well in bed with a twenty-sixer of straight malt scotch and a tall, cool woman with ebony hair and twilight grey eyes."

Jasper busied himself with the coat rack and glanced covertly at the hostess. She had heard, knew she was supposed to and ignored it as she was supposed to . . . with just a hint of nervousness. How is Angus going to get out of this one?

"Good evening, miss. Have you a table for two?" This said with no accent. The hostess was perceptibly surprised and habit took control before she could prevent it.

"Good evening, gentlemen. Yes, if you'll follow me."

Angus winked to Jasper and dug him painfully with an elbow. "*A Mhuire mhàthair!* She's a piece and a half, ain't she, bye?"

Again she heard and again she ignored it. Angus followed her down the aisle between the candlelit booths, his body moving from every joint in a great gesticulating leer. A **few** patrons smiled. Although he could not see Angus's face as they sat down, Jasper knew he had winked and whispered something to the hostess. She straightened her breasts into her close bodice and set a stony face as she walked away.

"Now there's a pair of dongs I'd like to get me sensitive surgeons fingers onto. Tart little bottom, too."

"She's wearing a girdle."

"We'll see about that."

"For God's sake, Angus."

"That's exactly why we'll see."

When the hostess returned with menus, she bent over the table. Jasper saw in Angus's eyes the devilish glint of certainty. The hostess moved away more quickly this time.

"No girdle?"

"No girdle." Angus leaned forward and whispered conspiratorially, "I think she's wearing those little bikini panties. I always wanted a pair as a souvenir."

"Angus, if you get them I'll have them framed for your wall and play my recorder all the way to Dartmouth on the ferry."

"She's a deal, bye."

They shook with absurd solemnity.

"You know, Jasper – and that's a bloody ridiculous name if I do say so – with those horn rims and the suit you look like a parson's son following his pa. But deacons don't carry wooden penny whistles in their coats. And what's in the parcel?"

"Ohh . . . just a pair of . . . galoshes."

"Well why the hell ain't you wearing 'em, bye?"

"They're a . . . present for a sick aunt who keeps budgies and can't leave the house to buy things for herself."

115

"We'll make a Cape Bretoner of ye yet, bye." And his laugh filled the restaurant.

Angus presented the party with a bottle of Rhine wine to go with the lobster and the chill of February lifted from them. The hostess stayed well away and they talked of mysticism. Jasper found that behind Angus's taurian face moved a brain of great brilliance. When two people converse on complex subjects, they need a set of common terms and a mutual acquaintanceship with certain forms of thought, certain short cuts. Jasper had been trained to these skills, Angus had not. Yet the Cape Bretoner had read widely and possessed a vocabulary rarely found except in zealous foreigners who memorize dictionaries. Most striking, however, was Angus's ability to make sudden unexpected transitions. The shallow-minded use such jumps to impress or confuse the listener with an implied depth of thought, but Angus was far too modest, far too confident for cheap tricks. The sparkle of his eyes changed from impudence to passionate mental struggle as he grappled with his ideas, forged them into words and presented them to Jasper with precision and proportion. He succeeded to an amazing degree, the ideas coming out like frozen crystals, clear, sharp edged, vibrant with light. Jasper found his own mind working as it had not done since those intense conversations far into the night of his second year at the University of Toronto. Black Angus was a brilliant man, a modest man, a man whose every word said, "This is how life can be lived . . . if you dare." Black Angus was what you had when you combined philosophy and guts.

"Port and cigars, bye?"

"Fine, fine."

"We'll have that cool one bring us the chaws and I'll see what progress I can make toward my side of the bargain."

When the hostess took the order for cigars, when she brought them, Jasper saw nothing happen. Angus was busy with McLuhan and Marcuse. Only when she came the last time did he notice Angus's gnarled finger touching the back of her hand as he reached for the bill. She paused an instant and Jasper knew the game was over.

He also knew he was gawking at the most beautiful woman he had ever seen and that he was hopelessly, irrevocably in love with her.

"Jasper, me bye, I suppose you're going to the men's, eh?"

"How long will you need?"

"I beg your pardon?"

"All innocence. I'll give you two minutes."

"Make it three; she's not your common harbour slut."

Turning at the entrance to the men's room, Jasper watched Angus saunter up the aisle with his hands in his pockets, timing his arrival at the counter to coincide with the return of the hostess from off in another part of the restaurant. That she would return was not in doubt. Jasper let the door sigh shut behind him.

In the street he said, "Well?"

"Well what, bye?"

Jasper did not answer. Suddenly Black Angus annoyed him. The obvious explanation was jealousy; this Jasper admitted readily. But he mistrusted easy answers. Because I don't like being teased? he wondered. Because he's not acting with due modesty? Or am I annoyed with myself for standing back and taking it? All these, all these paltry few and more . . .

"It's not easy, is it, bye?" Angus stopped and laid a hand on Jasper's sleeve. "It's like two freight trains meeting head on. Torn metal and mangled bodies, confusion and alarums. Where d'ye live, bye?"

"I have a room on Edward Street."

"How d'ye like it?"

"I don't."

"Likewise I'm sure and twice for the fiddler. Do you think we can stand each other's company in an apartment?"

"We could try."

Angus moved on, walking like an orang-utang; it was as if he had been an arboreal beast until twenty-one when he was given a human brain transplant and had spent the intervening five years marrying mind and body. The result was greater than the parts; out of the passion was born most violently a soul.

"Jasper, you are a man, aren't you? You have done things, tried and succeeded, tried and failed?"

Jasper felt at once completely at ease.

"I am a man."

"Well then, what the hell are we standing here for? I want to be moved in so's I'll have a pallet warm for Cecile by midnight." Heaven help me, Jasper groaned, what have I let myself in for?

BLACK ANGUS had them an apartment by nine o'clock. They hailed a cab to begin moving Jasper's belongings and Angus ordered it in the opposite direction. "Wanted to get to the Vendor's before she closed. Housewarming, you know." He made Jasper wait in the cab and returned with a case of a dozen bottles. "Black Diamond rum," he explained. "The Bluenoser's friend; keeps you warm in winter and cool in summer."

By plying the driver with rum, Angus arranged a flat rate of five dollars. "You're invited to the *ceilidh* of course, bye. And if you ever need a bed . . ." Bill had, they discovered, a shrewish wife. Jasper's gear required two trips and Angus's one. Except for two changes of clothes in a duffel bag, medical instruments in a satchel, he owned nothing but books. The three had finished a bottle of rum by the time the job was done.

"Well, byes, I have to be on me way now. D'ye prefer blondes, brunettes or redheads?"

Blondes, said the driver and redheads, said Jasper. Angus left them to their rum-soaked silence until after midnight when a knock sounded on the door. Jasper opened it to find a blonde and a redhead, both buxom, both eager.

"Hi," they chorused. "Is this where Black Angus is having the party?"

Jasper caught the Cape Breton accents and waved them in. Attempting to be jolly, he asked, "Are you from the Bay, bye?"

"No," they chorused. "We're from the Pier, dear."

They explained that the "Pier" was Whitney Pier near Glace Bay, that they were nurses just off evening shift who wanted some-

118

thing just like an Angus-party and they would both have Black Diamond, please. The blonde sat beside Bill; the redhead turned on Jasper's FM and managed to get him dancing. He no longer knew if the rum was in his brain or in the room; in the plush darkness he was aware only of a sensuous, affectionate feminine body clinging to his and a most sultry perfume drifting about him. After a time they decided to rest on the bed and the last thing he remembered was a throaty voice whispering that she was available anytime and call ward ten-east at the Victoria General.

Many hours later, another throaty voice whispered that he had a class. Waking was to pull his mind from the inner fastness of a bramble patch. Blood ran, wounds ached.

Because he could not find his robe, Jasper dressed before appearing for breakfast. He found Angus sipping coffee and wearing the bathrobe; Cecile, wearing one of Jasper's white shirts and very little else, was adoring her lover.

"Limited wardrobe, bye. Apologies."

Jasper mumbled and slipped into a chair before the most beautiful breakfast he had ever seen. Better gluttony than lust.

"You made a great hit with Janet." Angus pronounced the name as if he were Anglicising "Genet".

"Umf."

"She likes men who read books and belly dance."

"Umf?"

"Sure. Just after you did the can-can with her dress on. You don't remember?"

"Erk."

Angus tossed down his coffee and disappeared into the bedroom to dress. Jasper found himself eyeing Cecile who was eyeing something twenty feet above the ceiling. An angel, probably, best not disturb her. The trance did not end until she came to the door to kiss Angus good-bye. On the front doorstep Jasper sniffed the air. Thirty-three degrees and a promise of freezing rain. Yet it was somehow less dismal than the day before.

"D'ye really have a class, bye?"

"Sure."

"Shirr," Angus imitated. "Good guess, eh?"

"You were worried I'd make off with Cecile?"

"Not for a week yet. I just wanted her left alone. A woman is safe when she's confused and confused when alone."

"Thought you were a surgeon."

"Psychiatry should keep me in drinking money."

JASPER saw neither Cecile nor Angus for the next five days. He did not worry – how could one worry about Black Angus? – and guessed they were staying at Cecile's place for privacy and, no doubt, for comfort. His own was, to Jasper, just a shade better than the wretched single room he had forsaken.

The walls were cold plaster painted institutional green, the grimy windows covered with lace curtains so old they had probably been hung before the founding of Toronto. The house had once been a fine residence, perhaps for the province's top doctor or law-yer. A hundred years ago it would have contained over a dozen ele-gant rooms. Divided as it now was into six apartments and five single rooms, the building was no better than a stable with a human past. Due to some absurd architectural conceit in vogue when the house went up, Jasper and Angus's apartment on the second floor had been the kitchen. Their kitchen had been the pot closet, their bedroom the pantry. Jasper consoled himself with the knowledge that someone lived in the wine cellar.

And who does live here? he wondered. Lying in his bed over the weekend, Jasper listened to a continuing tattoo of high heels about the halls and stairways. The place was full of women. At a quiet hour on Monday morning he checked the mail and the bell-labels. Eighteen single women . . . plus himself and Angus. Angus had chosen the house; probably his idea of saving for a rainy day.

The list merely whetted Jasper's interest for more information. If he could find among them a quiet, beautiful, throaty-voiced fe-male who made wonderful breakfasts, who envisioned him in the form of an angel floating above her, whose name . . . whose name

120

was Cecile. Such a depressing situation; the ancient mariner and his water. Then who was the albatross? Ridiculous, ridiculous. In any case, Jasper listed the names and underlined the more interesting ones. There was Bo-bo Bobinski on the main floor, Margaret Rose Windsor down the hall from his own apartment, two Janes and a P.Q. Fleet above him and, in the wine cellar, A. Stubbs, B. Rhymer and C. Coates.

Names, just names. Where do the girls work? What do they look like? Where do they come from, where are they going? Which have boy-friends, which don't? Which ones dye their hair, which wear expensive perfumes? Which likes Mozart, which likes jazz and which plays country-and-western music all day long? So many questions, so many answers; and so much more interesting than a textual analysis of Beowulf variorum.

The girls seemed friendly enough. They knocked on his door to borrow cigarettes, they invited him for coffee, they chatted in the hall and greeted him warmly on the stairs. Jasper, of course, was pleased, but something worried him. "Hello," became "Hiii," accompanied by a pat on the cheek; subject matter during the chats grew increasingly intimate, and one afternoon four girls jostled him into a corner of the stairs where they made lewd whisperings into his ears. This cooled Jasper's curiosity and put him on his guard. Through the minimum opening of his door he rejected a judo lesson from the Janes on the top floor and a plea from Nikki Nott to approve the clothes she planned wearing on a date that night.

"What clothes?" he inquired suspiciously. "Why can't you come into the hall and let me watch from here?"

Nikki pushed futilely against the night chain. Her answer was evasive.

"Sorry, Nikki, I have to do a textual analysis of Beowulf variorum."

"Couldn't you do a whatever-it-is analysis of . . ."

The storm broke as he returned home one afternoon. After checking for mail – there was none – he stepped into the hall and heard:

"Hiii. Got a light."

She stood five and a half feet tall in the invitingly open doorway of apartment one. Long black tresses fell over her shoulders and onto her oversized bosom. Caught unawares, Jasper said, "Just a minute."

"I'll just hold your briefcase. Better still, I'll put it on the couch. My name is Bo-bo." The name trickled between two treacherously puckered lips.

As he returned to his senses, Jasper wished Angus were there: this creature was for real. With the cigarette an inch from the match, Bo-bo backed into the room.

"Which do you prefer, rum, gin, rye, scotch, vodka or beer? Hummm?"

"Well . . ."

"I had brandy until yesterday. But my room-mates drank it all. They just left for Bermuda for three weeks' vacation. I'm all alone."

"Here's . . . uhh . . . your light."

"You're Jasper, aren't you?"

The match was beginning to scorch Jasper's fingers when Bo-bo said, "The fellows who had the apartment before you moved out suddenly. I think they went to Dartmouth." As he struck another match, Jasper tried to recall the significance of "going to Dartmouth." Someone sometime had explained that it meant more than crossing to the city on the other side of the Harbour.

"Aren't you going to take your coat off?" called Bo-bo from the kitchen nook. The sound of pouring liquid reached Jasper's ears: she was filling with scotch a glass meant for beer. He was edging toward the door when he remembered the briefcase. As he reached for it, he glanced at the kitchen nook doorway and saw Bo-bo making naughty-naughty gestures from an ingeniously placed mirror.

"You're a student, aren't you? What do you study?"

"English."

"How marvellous! You have to read me some poetry . . . some love poetry." Bo-bo had apparently forgotten the drinks on the endtable, for she was easing Jasper toward the other end of the

122

couch. "Something . . . profane . . ." Her moued lips were poised above Jasper's drawn ones when a thunderous knocking sounded on the window.

"Well darn it, who could that be?"

Help? Reinforcements? The Morality Squad? Suddenly Jasper knew what it had been like at Mafeking the day of the Relief.

"Why it's Tom, Dick and Harry! You'll love Tom, Dick and Harry, they've been everywhere, seen everything, a barrel of laughs!"

Tom, Dick and Harry proved to be three exceptionally able seamen sailing with, Jasper saw from their hat ribbons, the HMCS *Venus,* They announced in chorus that they had just returned from three months of Naval exercises off Greenland and wanted a place to warm up.

"You've come to the right place," Bo-bo cried with glee. "And I suppose you'd all like rum?" she asked, darting into the nook. "And say hello to Jasper."

"Pleased to meetcha," growled Tom, extending an immense hairy paw. He was the big one.

"Any friend of Bo-bo's is a friend of ours," said Dick who was the sincere one.

"Unless he's in the bloody army!" laughed pudgy Harry, the funny one.

"How do you do . . . always wanted to meet a sailor . . ." He subtly manoeuvred Tom between the briefcase and the mirror and was just sliding out the door when Dick asked with concern, "Surely you don't have to leave already?"

Bo-bo was around the corner like a shot.

"Afraid . . . study . . . sorry . . . Beowulf variorum . . ."

"Studying? Are you a *bookie* or something?" Harry gasped before collapsing to the floor in laughter.

"Oh, Jasper, you promised to read me some poetry."

"Some . . . other time?"

"When the boys' shore leave is over in two weeks? I'll be waiting, Jasperrrr . . ."

Like a seasoned tar on the rigging, Jasper went up the stairs. Behind him erupted a sonata of giggles, guffaws and rumbles. His key was hardly in the slot when doors opened along the hall and heels sounded tentatively upon the stairs. Overcome by an orient of perfume, Jasper plunged. When the lock was locked and the chain chained and the bar barred, Jasper exhaled a sigh of relief. Then he remembered: "Going to Dartmouth" was a local euphemism for being committed to the mental hospital in that city. Halifax in February began to look like an entirely new and unexpected kind of hell.

ONLY WHEN the cathedral mind rests upon firm foundations can it vault thoughts of filigreed stone to spired heights. So much of Jasper's work was pure stodge, so little was flight, that he needed just peace and time and a sturdy desk with a lamp on it to get his degree. His friendship with Angus and his love of Cecile disturbed the peace, burned the time, wobbled the desk and extinguished the lamp. Jasper's eye developed a twitch.

On a Monday night toward the middle of February, Angus and Cecile and Jasper got drunk. The conversation began with anecdotes and ended many 80-proof hours later with Angus telling Jasper (Cecile having passed out) that, "This proves Attila the Hun was a bastard only because he had a stomach-ache from eating all that paprika." This was the last mutter Jasper heard until his alarm clock attacked his ear with a knitting-needle four hours later. When the clock was vanquished and demolished in a far corner, Jasper arose and mutely thanked God for a silent house.

Angus was already gone and Cecile still lay upon the chesterfield with one full breast peeping from under the covers. Jasper stood with his hand upon the doorknob; no thought, no feeling, no impression cracked his fragile brain. Painfully his gazed moved across the room and rested upon the galoshes. They had not yet been worn. Jasper knew intuitively that if he wore them everything would end, for he had acquired them the same day he acquired a friend and a beloved. So the galoshes sat in the corner.

Mind, companions, galoshes. All steady. Jasper was prepared for a day of comfortable stodge. A turn of the knob, two steps through the door and Jasper realized he had been in the eye of a hurricane.

"Hiii!"

"Girls, it's Jasper!"

"Flo, come and look!"

"My name is Velda!"

Every perfume in Paris, every eye-shadow of Hollywood, every dress of New York, every figure idolized by every sculptor from Praxiteles to Giacometti, every lovely face limned by every painter from Cimabue to Picasso swam before his eyes; a treacherous sea of beauty, Our Lady of the Sharks, sirens sweetly singing, mermaids melodiously murmuring, fingers like little fishes plucking at buttons and exposed bits of skin. Great God in heaven, he prayed, if You get me out of this one, I shall praise Thy works throughout my days and ways.

Then he plunged.

"There he goes!"

"He looks so wise with those horn-rimmed glasses!"

"He must be a professor!"

"What are you doing this evening?"

"What are you doing now?"

"Are you a professor?"

"I just adore Kafka!"

"Are you a Dostoevskian man, hummm?"

A Dostoevskian man! Why the hell wasn't Angus here? After all, these broads are his nest egg. Have I locked the door? What if they discover Cecile? They'll shred her and feed her to the sea gulls.

"He's going toward the university!"

"Let's offer him a ride!"

"No, we're going to drive him!"

"No, us, we saw him first!"

He was into a side street and through a backyard, over a fence, through a drugstore, along another alley-way, over two fences and,

with not a girl in sight, onto a trolley going the wrong way. He was safe.

FEBRUARY in Halifax destroys vision with a peculiar sort of illusion. With all colour grey and all light dim, the viewer sees every edge slightly blurred. To Jasper, returning in the afternoon, Cecile, as she stood in the battleship-grey Victorian doorway, sparkled like a diamond in the mud.

"Hi, Cecile."

"Ohh . . . hello."

"How . . . are you today?"

"Fine."

"Still breathing, eh? Ha-ha."

"Ha-ha."

"Umm."

"Ohh, Angus was in awhile ago. You're to meet him at the ferry wharf at sharp ten. And . . ."

"Bring my wooden penny whistle?"

"Yes, your wooden penny whistle."

"Yes . . ."

"Well . . . have to rush; I'm on at four."

"Yes . . . see you around."

"Yes. Toodle."

"Er . . . toodle."

Jasper raced a monkey up the stairs. The girls should all be at work, he knew, but from halfway along the block he had heard the giggles and squeals of Bo-bo Bobinski in ecstasy. You could never tell when she would tire of the undoubtedly prodigious though perhaps overly muscular charms of Tom, Dick and Harry and yearn for the academic dalliance of a man named . . .

"Jasper!"

Calm in the face of panic, Jasper caught himself before slamming the door, easing it to instead. Ever so quietly he locked the lock, chained the chain and barred the bar. He had recently added some six inch spikes; these he twisted across the door before collapsing onto his bed. He set the alarm for nine-thirty, remembered food and reset it for eight-thirty, then crawled under the covers where he stared at the uniformly dismal ceiling until he fell asleep at twenty five minutes after eight.

"ACH, BYE, it's a damn shame you tore your pants, but why were you coming down the fire escape in the first place?"

"Sixteen ravenous women smouldering in the halls. They wouldn't have known I was there if Bo-bo hadn't opened her big yap . . ."

"Bo-bo! Now there's a piece and a half, bye. I still have the welts on my back . . ."

"Angus, have you been at those broads already?"

"Just inventorying the stock. Not a bad apple in the lot, though I don't know about Bo-bo's room-mates. They're in Bermuda . . ."

"I know and thank God for that."

"Ach, well, so you've been tasting of the forbidden fruit . . ."

Over the harbour hung a fine mist dank with fish and tar. Angus led the way to the top deck where he borrowed Jasper's newspaper for a seat cover.

"Avast and ahoy!" called Angus. "Gun the manboats and scuttle the scuppers." The whistle blew an extended blast just behind Jasper's ear and a thrumming began deep below them. "Batten the binnacles, the keel is awash and the bosun's gone for a poop!"

Jasper took out his recorder and began his Henry viii piece while Angus danced. After a minute he took a pint of rum from his back pocket, swilled a great draught and passed the bottle to Jasper.

"D'ye have to stop, bye?"

"If I'm to drink it."

"Next time I'll pour it down the reed and you can blow pretty bum-rubbles in the air."

As the music resumed, Angus clattered about the deck, his arms and feet flapping like the wings of a great bird, tragically, absurdly unable to fly.

"D'ye know, bye, I'm the seventh son of a seventh son. For a

Cape Bretoner it's a sure mark of greatness. The old people point to me in the street and the young ones are a bit shy of me. There's a word for it in the Gaelic, but I don't ha' much o' the tongue. I'll have to get about learning it one of these days."

The tempo of the music decreased slightly.

"What are ye thinking man, what? Tell me what ye're thinking, Jasper, for we're friends and it's a desolate sea all around with nothing but the heart to warm it."

"More rum."

"Smash 'er down for I've another boh'le in me harse pocket. But come over to the rail and look at the world from the centre of Halifax Harbour. What does it mean to you, bye?"

Jasper felt overpowered by fatigue. The light of the two cities glimmering through the mist and reflected in the water was so obvious; Angus wanted him to force some obscure symbolism from it.

"Ach, bye, I see how obvious it is. Direct light from the cities and the suspension bridge is like a wall of light; that's our world. The light in the water falls like a curtain into the abyss. Then you make a transference: the wall above is the real, the celestial; the curtain below is the unreal, the material. A psychologist would take the wall as the conscious, the curtain as the unconscious. A theologian would . . . but the hell with theology. I'm here to tell you a *sgeulachd,* a story, if you'll listen. Of how I lived Halifax Harbour."

Nice of him to give me the choice, Jasper thought. "Sure," he replied.

"But you do have the choice," Angus breathed. He leaned over the rail and Jasper found himself doing the same. Damn him, he can even make me relax when I don't want to. The seventh son of a seventh son should be kept outside fences . . . but that wouldn't be much fun, would it?

"Tell me your story."

WELL BYE, she happened the first year I came to the big city. Of course, I'd been to New York, Boston, Frisco, Vancouver, Montreal, Toronto, but I'd never lived there. Halifax was the big town.

129

The other freshmen considered me a bit of an *enfant terrible* and I suppose I was. Give a Bay bye six hundred dollars in his harse pocket and he figures half of it goes on rum and to hell with living expenses. I was five sails to the breeze and steering by the stars when the football game started on Initiation Saturday. A frat gave an open house after the game so I burned my beanie, slipped another mickey into me pocket and away I went.

Through the madding crowd I caught a glimpse of a tall, smart-looking girl, casually dressed but in clothes that would take a chop out of Queen Elizabeth's wardrobe budget. She had a glass and a cigarette in one hand and the hand bent back in a way that's called effeminate on men and sophisticated on women. Long, natural blonde hair – I'm enough of a small town bye that I still like natural hair – and her head thrown back in laughter. Thinnish face – she'd be horsy at forty – all very chic.

D'ye have that picture frozen in your mind? Small town Angie remembers it to this day. Just the kind of cool rich bitch we all slobber after and never try . . . except that I had the rum and the arrogance in me.

Of course, the complication in all these cases is the Prince Charming beside her. President of the frat, captain of this, chairman of that, comes from Montreal where his old man owns a distillery or something. Drives a low little car with more horses under the hood than there are drays on Cape Breton Island. Big man on campus.

So I elbowed me way through the crowd and stood about ten feet from her across an open space between two rooms. Me in me clodhoppers and jeans and a new white shirt open halfway down me chest. I pulled down the eyebrows like a wool cap and growled to meself for effect.

She was a sharp one, no doubt about that. She had seen me, sized me and cut me dead two seconds after I began the stare. It couldn't have been much worse. But I kept on, trying to make her uncomfortable while figuring a new approach. Obviously it'd have to be something new – she'd have heard them all before. Something, say, so absurd she'd fall laughing into my arms. So I took a long pull on the rot-gut, dusted off the knuckles and walked over. Ignoring Miss Icicle, I says to Prince Charming:

"Ah-ha, Plimpstone-Coriander, you see your nemesis has caught you up at last! Yes, 'tis I, Beaufort de Montresor de Montresoris, returned from the slave galleys! Take that, you cad!"

His "What the . . ." was squashed by a pile-driver to the point of the chin and he went across fifteen feet of floor and crashed through a window. One down and twenty to go – you see, he really was the pres. of the frat. Confusion was the only chance, so I shoved a few by-standers and yelled "Get the dirty bastards!" It helped that lots of Saint F. X. fans were there from the game. Haymakers were flying six ways from Sunday. I was at work with me Judique boxing-gloves while looking the other way and marvelling at the beauty of those mainland *cailleachan* handing it out like pit men. Right out of a cowboys and Indians movie and that was absurd enough. I waded through the mob looking for Her and found her – with the hand still cocked – in a corner dodging the bodies. I picked her up like a baby calf and walked out the door.

"Let me down, you great bloody ape!" she cries.

"Can you run?" I asks.

"In the opposite direction. Let me . . ." She still had some spirit.

"Not bloody likely. I'm abducting you to my mountain lair where I shall ravish you in a fit of uncontrolled passion."

Down a side street and through an alley and she was still on tight and starting to cry. I unloosed me right paw and clipped her across the puss. She wept more quietly so I let her down beside a garage and poured on the tenderness.

"Why are you doing this to me?" she weeps. "Who are you?"

"I'm Black Angus MacDonald and I think you're the most beautiful woman in the world. I'm going to chain you to a bed and hump you till you hump me in return. Then I'll send you back to Prince Charming and never speak to you again."

I got her to her feet and led her along to Citadel Hill. It was getting dark but the breeze was warm off the ocean. I made her wipe the blood from my face and although the haughtiness returned, she did begin to see the humour of it all.

"I suppose you think I'm a professional virgin and you're going to rescue me from a fate worse than death?"

"You have the most beautiful hair, silken as a sea-breeze."

"You think you can make me laugh and forgive you for being a beast?"

"Your nape is soft with down as some wild creature caught in a cruel snare."

"You think that just because you're handsome and rock-jawed I'll fall like a ton of bricks?"

"Your calves are slim and firm as if turned on a heavenly lathe by Hephaestus himself."

"You think I'm a frigid rich bitch who just needs a good lay to make her human."

"Your thighs are smooth and creamy as . . ."

"Get your hands off my thighs!"

So I tumbled her over and kissed her until she came up laughing and things went on from there. When the night was cooler I took her down for a bite to eat. Of course she was cow-eyed by this time and I had discovered that, although she was witty, she was just slightly more intelligent than a sledge-hammer. Not an awfully good lay, either. I was wondering how to get rid of her without having her daddy buy me off for a block of blue chip and a one-way ticket to Tasmania. It came to me over the rum parfait that I oughta go along with the stream of things and "stream" reminded me of water and "water" of the Harbour. I led her down to the depot, laid two dimes on the man and we sailed away into the ferry-land night.

ANGUS STOPPED talking. They had reached the Dartmouth side and passengers were loading for the return trip. As before, Angus and Jasper were left alone on the open top deck. Well out into the harbour again, Angus made a gesture – Gaullic rather than Gaelic – and stood back from the rail.

"What happened then?"

132

"Ach bye, the plot thickens, of course. I'm no damn artist, don't you know. That's what you have to be to tell a story you don't understand yourself."

"Tell me the events."

Angus covered his face with his hands a long minute.

"Ach well, the events, then. We came to the rail, about here and I looked out and saw the wall and the curtain and the abyss. My mind went black. She said nothing for a long time until she touched my arm and said, 'Angus?'

"I broke into tears. I cried all the way over and all the way back, then in the taxi to her residence and back to me room and so until I fell asleep.

"I saw her on campus sometimes and we smiled or nodded. Never spoke. I had some trouble with Prince Charming and his jaw – had to rough a few of his frat brothers in dark alleyways for a few weeks – but nothing else. She married him, I think . . . I don't know."

ONE MORNING Jasper awoke to find Cecile's face two inches from his own. He recalled a story told by an uncle who had served in Burma who had come awake with a cobra on his chest. "The problem, my boy, was to get hold of my bayonet without the reptile seeing me move . . ." Jasper reassured himself that his own world was more or less at peace.

"Angie said you were to be roused at ten."

"Umm . . . Where's himself?"

"Himself is gone. You know how it is."

"Umm . . . You're very beautiful."

"I bet you say that to all the girls."

"Only the beautiful ones. Get out of my room so I can get dressed."

Here she is, mused Jasper over his coffee, this warm, wonderful woman, Black Angus's woman. Angus would say she was mine for the taking because he'd do the same. Go ahead, he'd say, take her, just you bloody well try to take her. She's all yours. Except I'll scoop out your tripes with a rusty spoon. And he'd do it, too. Just as he'd expect me to do the same in reverse except that he's the seventh son of a seventh son from Cape Breton and he always gets to hold the spoon.

"Cecile, why are you with Angus?"

"Because he's Angus."

"Correct. What do you expect from him?"

"Some of his time, some of him, some memories."

"Correct. You assume, though, that he'll leave you?"

"I don't think about it. There's only now."

"You have just passed Phil 1. What about me?"

"You?"

"What are you to me, what am I to you?"

"Friends of Angus."

"Time I was getting off to class. Bye-bye."

"Toodle . . . Jasper."

"Ohh . . . toodle."

This scene was repeated the next morning with almost the same words. Jasper tried to kiss Cecile while she hovered above him. She dropped a kindly smile on the little boy and stuck a glass of orange juice in his face. On the morning of the nineteenth, Jasper's spirits reached the high point of the month when Cecile allowed him to touch her cheek. The touch lasted less than a second, but progress is sometimes slow. Then, miracle or miracles, the same day as he was going out the door she said,

"By the way, tonight is my night off and you're to take me somewhere."

"I am?"

"By orders of himself. I don't know where, but he'll phone instructions later. Can you be home by six?"

"Yes."

"And wear your galoshes; I don't want you missing it because you have pneumonia."

"I can't."

"Funny Jasper."

134

"Toodle."

"Toodle."

WHILE AT U of T, Jasper had missed a room-mate's wedding because he was studying and forgot what time it was. On the afternoon of the nineteenth of February, Jasper was so concerned with being on time that he did not study at all. Instead, he sat in the dismal canteen drinking cup after cup of coffee in a chair which allowed him to cross-check his watch with the electric clock every five minutes. People came and went. Jasper craved a beer but didn't move. At last he decided to go home at five instead of six. This meant leaving at four-thirty. At twenty after four he pulled on his coat. At twenty-five-after he left, trying not to make himself ridiculous by running, for he was a graduate student in whom solemnity is becoming.

As he approached his street through the gathering gloom, Jasper remembered the women, those crazy women who wanted him, those frenzied bacchantes hunting out a victim. Bo-bo's sailors had been taken off the day before when her room-mates returned from Bermuda. As the Navy ambulance pulled away, a Shore Patrol jeep took its place. Burly, truncheon-carrying meat-heads went in to Bo-bo's to investigate. The jeep was still there in the morning. But would they be enough?

The fire escape entrance had been successful in its time, but would be useless in the dying light. And the girls would be watching. He would have to pass the side of the house, past the door to the basement apartment where resided the gorgeous, ravenous and stupid A. Stubbs, B. Rhymer and C. Coates. If he came over the back fence . . . but he had tried that last night and was spotted before his legs came into view by P.Q. Fleet and the two Janes on the top floor. It was a race between Jasper going up and P.Q. and the Janes coming down. Only a stroke of luck saved him: the upper section broke and the three girls were tumbling past in the air as he dived through his kitchen window. Unhurt, they were back up and leering after him as he pulled the curtains to.

But that was yesterday. Today he would need more luck, more agility, more ingenuity altogether. He might try leaping from the adjoining house . . . swinging in via rope . . . dressing as a girl for a frontal assault . . . dressing as the man come to read the meters . . . Passing a corner smoke-novelty shop, Jasper's anxious gaze fell upon a garish little ad in the style of the thirties advertising "Skunk Water! The World's Worst Smell! Disgust your friends . . . unwanted salesmen . . . the dog next door . . ."

TEN MINUTES later Jasper staggered into his apartment amid a cacophony of outraged wails.

"Congratulations, Jasper, you've won again."

"Be a dear, Cecile and run me a hot bath. And keep the bathroom door closed; I want every molecule of steam. Perhaps that way . . ."

"It is ghastly, isn't it. How are your feet?"

"Soaking wet, as usual."

"Funny Jasper."

She ran the water and he was soon settled deep in the porcelain womb. After a knock, Cecile's hand came through the door with a glass of hot lemonade.

"For your pneumonia."

"My God, Cecile, I adore you."

"I know Jasper, but you still haven't a chance."

"Drat the luck."

A FOG enveloped Jasper – whether inside or outside his skull he did not know. When the ringing of a telephone had died away he held his hand before his face and waited for it to focus. After a lengthy and minute examination he saw that it was corrugated; long after this he found that his whole body was corrugated. Horrors! He had been trapped inside the skin of an albino elephant; the natives meant him as a ritual sacrifice followed by a cannibalistic orgy . . .

"Jasper, supper's ready."

He was unable to answer.

"Come on, Jasper, up and at 'em."

Could it be that the natives had stuffed his mouth with an enormous snail? Was he to be served as suckling Jasper?

"Jasper? . . . Jasper, are you all right? . . . Jasper? . . . Jasper . . . My God, the fool has slit his throat!"

Into the bathroom she rushed, the high priestess of the glutton cult. At least, Jasper observed, these cults know how to pick them. Why she looks like . . .

"Jasper? Are you alive? What have you done to yourself?"

Habit came to Jasper's rescue. There before his eyes – not two inches away – was the face of Cecile. Then he wasn't to be sacrificed, he was not in the power of a glutton cult, it had all been a bad dream. Femininity, Woman, Eve, Venus, Pygmalion (or was it Galatea?), Cecile, wearing three-inch heels, standing on a bedewed bathroom floor and already extended to the limits of her balance was easily brought to terms by Jasper's weakened arms.

"Come into bed with me Cecile, I love you so much, I would climb the highest mountain or swim the broadest ocean . . ."

The waters parted to let Cecile in; half the volume went over the side. When the waters rushed together over her, they rose to a magnificent crown and half the remainder went over the side. The two might have drowned in what was left had it not been absorbed in its entirety by Cecile's clothes. Jasper helpfully manoeuvred her to the bottom where her dress swabbed up the few non-conformist drops.

"Oh, Cecile, Cecile, I love you more than all the stars in the sky, than all the fish in the sea . . ."

Cecile's hand went out in search of something, anything to aid her. Into its grasp came a plumber's friend. With laudable adroitness considering the awkwardness of her position, she succeeded in raising it in the air and bringing it down upon Jasper's head.

"Cecile, (thump) Cecile, say you'll (thump) be mine (thump) my darling, my (thump) dearest (thump) . . ."

WHEN THE FLOOR was sponged dry, when Cecile had changed her clothes, set and dried her hair, when Jasper was dressed and fed and the back of his head shaved and disinfected and bandaged, when the very air of the apartment seemed again sane and quiet, then did Jasper manage to say in a hoarse and hesitant voice:

"Please forgive me, Cecile."

"That's all right, Jasper. It's kind of funny when you look back on it. I'm sorry about clubbing you like that, but a girl has a reputation to protect . . ."

Jasper blushed deeply. "I suppose it's pleasant to know I'm a clubbable man."

"Good grief! But you promised to take me to the party, remember?"

"You mean you're still going with me?"

"I'm going with you but I'm meeting Angus. Don't you remember that? But let's go. We have to buy the liquor and the Commission closes soon. And Jasper, will you wear your galoshes, please, at least so your feet won't drip all over the carpet when we get there."

"But . . ."

"Wear them for me?"

"Will you kiss me if I do?"

"Well . . . once, lightly."

"A deal. The kiss first?"

"No."

"Please?"

"Well . . ."

So Jasper and Cecile kissed, once lightly, and he staggered across the room to where, under an expensively framed pair of black bikini panties, sat his shiny new galoshes.

"I STAND BEFORE this . . . mirror . . . to confront mine own . . . image," said Jasper aloud. "Yet mine own image is smudged and blurred. This blurred . . . effect is no doubt in part due to the twenty-four ounces of rum in which my brain now floats like a sponge, but also in part to a layer of smudge on the glass. I cannot see myself because of both an inner and an outer distortion of the vision. There should be a profundity, but I don't see the profundity. Where the hell is Black Angus Ma'Donald to 'splain it to me? Where's he? Where?"

Black Angus was not in the bathroom. Jasper knew this but checked anyway. After some time he unlocked the door and stumbled back to the party where, because the sun was rising behind the cloud banks over the world, only a few guests remained. Beside Angus and the adoring (if sleepy) Cecile, four couples remained.

"Ye look lonely, bye. Where's that woman gone? The big redhead?"

"Don't tease him, Angie, he's had a hard night, haven't you Jasper?"

"Umm."

"That's the spirit."

"Well look, bye, don't just say something, sit there."

"Umm."

"D'ye know ye're lying?"

"Angus, tell me about perception by mirror image."

"Ach bye, I cried all the way home."

"Umm . . ."

"Jasper," said Cecile in a kindly voice, "why don't you go home? The party is almost over . . ."

"He's not to go home. Our lonely Upper Canadian has not yet learned to take an epic view of things. Jasper, siddown for a few minutes, rest your mind."

"Angus, don't be so cruel to him. Poor Jasper has been up almost twenty-four hours."

"Ach, I've been going fifty-three and I'm on duty in virology lab at nine."

"That's different."

"Shut your face woman, Jasper wants to know about mirrors."

Seeing it was useless, Cecile relapsed into adoration while Angus rambled on about mirrors, back and forth, in and out, making

139

mirrors himself. Jasper listened numbly. Angus was just hammering up his conclusion with spikes of bone and mallets of mind when a knock, a great uproarious pounding sounded at the door.

"Answer it, Jasper me bye, I'm occupied at the moment."

Jasper hated leaving in the middle of an argument, but he had been lost at the first inverted Cape Breton syllogism, so he arose. As his hand turned the knob, certain phrases, certain memories, certain somethings in his mind turned minutely and he felt he should know what was on the other side of the door. Had he been granted ten hours sleep and a few seconds calculation he might have guessed. This, however, was not the case. He opened the door and in poured eighteen beautiful, ravenous and stupid women, led by Bo-bo herself (and her room-mates returned from Bermuda), followed by the Janes, P.Q., A., B., C., and all the others.

"Jasper!"

"How nice of you to invite l'il ol' us!"

"Were you talking about Hegel just now?"

"Who's Hegel?"

"My name is Velda!"

"I just adore Kafka!"

"Are you a Dostoevskian man, humm?"

Angus was laughing a wild and frightening laugh, a chthonic laugh from the coal-black depths; Cecile, knowing the situation was hopeless, continued adoring; among the other couples, only one body stirred, the movement being a hand toward an empty rum bottle.

"Have to . . . the john . . . whole boh'le . . . barf all over you if you . . . don't . . ."

He lost only a sleeve from his sport coat while escaping. Once down the hall and around the corner, he dashed for the kitchen where the coats and boots lay in an unsegregated heap.

Got to get out of here . . . Halifax in February just insane . . . back to room on Edward Street sleep off the month (today the twentieth – nine days left) . . . no more Black Angus, no more Bo-bo and P.Q. A. B. C. . . . Where's my coat? . . . here, and the galoshes?, oh yes, hid them in a corner here they are shiny new with just a bit of slush worth a kiss from Cecile (Oh! radiantly beautiful Cecile!) and . . .

"Great God, someone has taken my right galosh! Someone has left me a left galosh! Who stole my right galosh?"

"Down this way girls, he's trying to get out the back way!"

"Stop!"

"Halt!"

"Head him off at the pass!"

"Jasper! Jasperrr!"

"My name is Velda, do you hear me, Veldaaa . . ."

Not far from the house where the party was held is a field named Gorsebrook Field. Once, presumably, it had been a farm; later it was part of a golf course; now it is just an incongruously large field with some trees and a school at one end, another school and a clump of trees at the other end. That grey morning as February moved into Pisces, Gorsebrook Field lay covered in sordid snow. In the lower part of the field the snow was saturated from beneath and was, in fact, a quagmire of slush. If we were to stand atop the hill and look down at this slush, if we were to squint our eyes to close off the outer edges of the picture, we should see a background of grey, unbroken except for a small black figure in the lower left-hand corner. It is cut in the rough, the sharp-edged shape of a man running. One leg is touching the ground and bent slightly at the knee; the other lifted beside it and bent to a greater angle. That is the picture frozen before our eyes. The man running is Jasper. There is no place in Halifax in February for a man with two left feet.

The Dwarf in his Valley Ate Codfish

I. THE GREAT MAN. Long noses and petulance; the Great Man himself used to sit here, but that was in the old days when things were not as they are now. Is it a sense of loss we feel? Yes, I believe so, for we are weak. I do not like a south wind blowing.

There are many things to forget. See, here, carved into the doorstep: "ME". Neat lettering, deep, straight and with every serif in fine proportion, to commemorate the night the buffalo passed by, surly and awesome, a shadow and a rumble. *You* remember!

Make a vista for yourself; I will not disturb it; I am going round to the back of the house to the trees. Come if you wish, or not as also you wish. I will not trouble you.

I'm glad; one worries about proportion.

I have always wanted power; I begin to fear I have not got it in me. Oh yes, at times, under some circumstances, but always artificial. We ponder the fate of the codwife and her dark lover . . .

Put your nose in this shed; we remember it from back over the (so many!) years. It was in there that we played the rumple game. How did it go? Yes. After all, what else can you do with a daffodil? You have a sleek sense of humour, sliding otter jokes that end with a splash. Ah! The tyranny of delight!

I see horses, one flesh-coloured, one lime green, two red and two orange and the second orange one is leaping over a lime green sawhorse. It has not moved in six years. Beyond that (beyond the six years) I cannot (would not) vouch for it. Perhaps the Great Man . . . but that is no matter. Not *now*.

Was Alexander the Great's horse called Bucephalus? I have a feeling he was. History lacks sincerity; so I have always thought. The Great Man once accused history of three crimes, none of which was committed in the name of passion. The magistrate tossed the case out of court for lack of evidence. This tree will mean something to you . . .

Curious, doubtless, I never knew. But then, there is so much one never knows. Don't you find that so? I once saw a falcon and thought myself lucky. If you enquire into the history of playing cards you will find, I surmise, that the Queen of Spades has always been evil . . .

Utopian characters always play a local variation of chess, inferior because of the writer's blind spots. But think! Think of the wildman or the fascinating mystery of Basilisk-Thorpe at Arras in '93. But then, even I sing at times for no reason at all. Yes.

Save string.

Fatuity is excusable for the same reason that sincerity is insufferable; it all depends upon the bending of the reeds when, under the scudding clouds, the wind comes in over the marshes, nervous, chill, agéd . . .

The long grass . . . I once thought happiness was balanced tension but the nostrum is no longer of much use to me. That does not make it less true – you'll recall the crow and the rune.

Have a lemon . . . go ahead. No lemon groves o'erhang the hoary Don. Did you know (you who have loved a red-haired girl) that one half of an oyster shell has a black spot on it? At the age of seven, right here (or there, or wherever you wish) I put a bullet through an oyster shell about half an inch from the bull's-eye. The shell (of the oyster) is still around; I think it is in one of those cupboards you browse through on a rainy day. Old books, chocolate boxes full of trinkets, etc.

Red and blue stripes: that is the key.

Say something.

Plantagenet.

Codfish.

Nettles.

There's a political pun to be made out of Caesar's crossing the Rubicon; I can't be bothered explaining it for it is complicated and, I expect, of little interest to any but me.

Fol-de-ree

Fol-de-ray

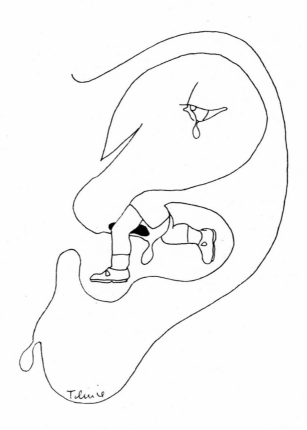

Turn a key

End the day.

One sometimes wonders about dimensions. He did, frequently . . . mused upon the difference between weight and specific gravity . . . made several cunning observations. Or: consider a planet. Yes, exactly, the Great Man said as much himself numerous times.

He looked into the alcove (the buffalo again) and thought to himself: any God worth a damn would surely have the sense of humour to put up real red, white and blue-striped north and south poles. Well, he said, really, I don't think it's too much to ask, after all, he said, the agéd pederast once . . .

Thus (or so) the Agéd Pederast:

An old room, very old, with small sooty windows, old *objets d'art* from years past (why the past itself!) cluttered about. The fireplace doesn't draw well. In his worn chair sits the agéd pederast reading a pornographic book. The pederast is snickering; he wipes the saliva from his chin with a dirty, hardened handkerchief . . . We steal closer . . .

Possibly. I'm not sure.

What is it about marzipan? There's something about marzipan. You can't trust people with pens.

"France, Spain, Italy, Germany, Poland, Russia, Sweden, Turkey, / Arabia, Palestine, Persia, Hindostan, China, Tartary, Siberia, /" – the feet upon the endless stair – "Egypt, Lybia, Ethiopia, Guinea, Caffraria, Negroland, Morocco, / Congo, Zaara, Canada, Greenland, Carolina, Mexico, / Peru, Patagonia, Amazonia, Brazil: . . ." You quote from the bard.

Have a handkerchief, his nose is running.

Wouldn't it be great, she thought, to be a walrus! (I have a friend who is happy much of the time.)

No, not you, of course . . . We wonder what to do about the Beautiful and so we draw maps showing holes in the ground; but when we try to use the maps the holes have unaccountably moved. Holes do that.

See . . . there . . . a man on crutches.

Now the Great Man used to be brought out here in the evenings to . . . listen I suppose. He was blind as a bat by then, but the
ears of a bat too. The women used to say it was so touching, but
women always say that sort of thing. See, here is the trailing arbu-
tus; it was his favourite flower for some reason unknown to the rest
of them. Here, have a collander. No, really, I have a whole carton in
my room.

Yes, all right. Perhaps we could wear sweaters as I know your
dislike for clouds which assume the shape of earthly objects.

I beg your pardon?

Possibly; in any case, I'm off to the beach now. Think upon the
broken pillar and the goatherd's jolly song.

Harrooo . . .

II. GLADYS. Gladys: but then she never knew the difference. You wonder sometimes, you really wonder how long, how long O! Israel.
You can try erasing but the whole web is ersatz. It's like trying to ex-
tract minutes from yesterdays. She had style; she also had long hair.
The hair probably explained more. I don't know.

"So," he said and walked down the mountain. What the hell
can you do, he asked himself, what can anyone do about panoramas? He just walked down the mountain until he came to a tavern
and he went into the tavern and got drunk. No one cared. They did-
n't even ask him for money. You don't care, he yelled, you don't give
a damn. What the hell do I have to do, expose myself? (It was one of
those countries.)

So he exposed himself and no one gave a damn.

Gladys! Gladys! he cried and they turned away. Out in the street
his feet tended naturally on down the mountain. God knows what
happened to him after that. Perhaps we'll find out later. I wasn't
there at the time, but I heard it from someone or other. It is substan-
tially true.

You were sitting at the far end of the long table (so elegant) and
I could hardly see you because the candles were the only light in the

room and you said to me, "Marjorie, this is the damndest best bouillabaisse I've ever tasted," and I thought about it not having *racasse,* which you can't get here. When w*as* that? I remember the glitter; there was at least as much inside me. But I don't know; what are you supposed to say about crimes of this sort? Are they really crimes? Perhaps that's more to the point. We talk about Macedonian blood feuds that were ageless when Alexander the Great was counting his fingers for Aristotle, we talk about *wergeld* and we can go to an art gallery and see paintings worth a king's ransom. So.

Take for example a fellow I knew in the army. Mashie-Niblick was his name. An officer and a gentleman, a really despicable piece of humanity. He got himself cashiered for gambling debts and, having learned his role well from a lot of chintzy pot-boilers, never got back up again. Finally hung himself from a sconce by his regimental tie. It was pretty silly, really, he was eighty-seven at the time. I believe he was afraid of lightning.

In any case, this is the lino print block. I suppose it should have been destroyed but my wife restrains me. He listened to the radio a lot while Gladys was still alive and she thought he was in love with me. "Marjorie," she would say, "he has to be in love with you, you're so much more beautiful." Although I wasn't really, just more photogenic. Gladys could never see the difference. I mean, she never wore a girdle and I think men adored her for that. I tried not wearing one but it just didn't work, I have these solid, child-bearing hips. It was the same even when I was young enough that it mattered. In any case here is, as I said, the lino print block.

Gladys, Gladys: I always loved her, I always feel that when she dies the world will end. It was cool and bright the morning he set out. The only sounds were birdsong and the rustling of the dew. Clear, so clear! and bright. He sang a song as he walked along and the song he sung was "The Bottom Rung". (And ring it did . . . later.) There's nothing like beginning a journey; we've all done it. It was a shame his ended so quickly and so tragically. Ten girls in the county swore they never would marry and at least one, the ugliest and stupidest, was able to keep her threat. Revelation is the bread of

fools, the bane of merchants, and the salve of kings. So much for bloody journeys.

Take this street, for instance. Fifty years ago it was nothing but a quaggy swamp. Progress, they say, marches on. But when you're my age you find your mind back in that swamp. The swamp harboured wildfowl, doubtless, and there were sedges of one sort and another. The world should make a place for bogs. Yes, I mean that, in spite of what happened to Gladys. You see, in spite of it all, she wasn't too bright. Midnight wanderings: well really, now, what can you expect?

Once I was sitting in a bleak tavern. It was the wrong time of day and the only other person there (besides the arthritic barmaid who appeared every now and then) was a rather dispirited prostitute doing a crossword puzzle. She had propositioned me earlier in a sadly apologetic way and I had thanked her, apologetically no. We chatted a bit about the weather while she chipped away at her memory. Then she asked me for a six-letter word for "yoke" beginning with "z". I said, "Zeugma," and she said, no, it wasn't a Polish crossword. We got it worked out after a while. The funny thing – macabre if you wish – was that it was in this very tavern that Gladys had first met Stanislaus Zeugma, her – shall we say? – fate . . .

Or, see that fellow just going into that house across the street . . . yes . . . well, he wears a chastity belt . . . yes, voluntarily . . . and his wife is a prostitute too. It's all over the place but it's keeping me alive because it's milled from washed wheat.

She liked gambling a lot and was rather good at it. So it was with some misgivings that I heard them ask her, "Hey Margie, how about a game of strip poker?" There were six men and just her and when the game was over she was fully clothed. After she had teased us a bit she took off too. She was always a good sport which is why, I think, everyone disliked her so much. She disliked artichokes.

I remember Gladys at school; she was the cause of much violence. Old Nosey's life was ruined by the scandal. It was then we saw she was utterly amoral. Doorways meant nothing to her. It's infuriating, you see; you work and work building something and at the

151

very last minute you find out you've used water instead of glue. (You wonder what happened to the glue and then you brush your teeth . . .) Oh yes, she had a way about her. If only she hadn't giggled so much.

"Why?" he yelled when he had emerged from the sewer. "Why?"

"Who wants to know?" they called back.

"A wayfaring stranger."

"Screw strangers."

And so. Usually they were an hospitable bunch but you'd be unwise to depend on it. Oh, he stumbled about, muttering, trying as we all do to find a dignified out, but all he came up with was Gladys' name. So he took another swig from his bottle and cried, "Gladys . . . Gladys!" As he should have expected, they tore him apart and fed him to the dogs. That was the sort of effect she had on people. The morning the duel was to be fought she said to me, "Margie, I deserve this, don't I?" and I replied, "Gladys, you sure do." It seemed to make her happy; God knows, she needed happiness.

III. THE SHADOW PEOPLE. I remember the one with the artificial breasts saying how deep do you have to go anyway? Isn't there a limit? I mean . . . She crossed her legs so that her skirt rode up, the exposure giving her as much pleasure as it gave us. The secret, she once told Madelaine, is an aura of prurience. Along with her perfume she wore some secret scent with aphrodisiacal qualities. We found out later it was a drop of fish oil.

It just goes on. The frightening part of it is that nothing gets added, but things die and get taken away until there's nothing left but the going on. Process is horrible. But there are still hedgehogs. Remember the hedgehog; consider the hedgehog; venerate the hedgehog. So also:

Codfish

Cauliflowers

And Mira the Wonderful.

Here, you can't do that . . . Really, though, in a place like this we'll have no stories about altarboys and streetlights. I've heard them all anyway. Try one about the raven.

Take the Marianas Trench, for e.g.; you can't go a hell of a lot deeper than that. Or in people, is the sole or the soul deeper? or the gut? Or how many fish live deeper than the sole, as if that solved anything. What a lot of nonsense; there's nothing more meaningless than connections.

That far under the water there was no light and he found himself feeling his way along the stainless steel wall, his fingers probing for a break, a turning. It was not much after that his brother found a moose head in the piano and an unnamed girl, dressed in white, looked up and down the street before stepping into a dark doorway. It went on like that day after day until the old man died. His last request was for a kipper and when they said he shouldn't eat kippers in his condition he bawled at them, "Not to eat, you fools, to look at. Bah!" And so expired.

The question he was putting to them was this: Why can't it all happen on a seashore? You have your eel-grass, your driftwood, waves, sea urchins, rocks, wind, sky, weather, sea . . . Hell, what else is there? Run it up over a dune and add some sex and there you are. To hell with formalizations; to hell with inlaid ceilings and pillars; what the hell do they matter? He was a brash young fellow, they said, and you know what they're like. J. D. (going under the name of A. C.) once told the feeble crow to go castigate the rood. People listened to him, though, because whatever he said had the heft of an anvil.

Once she got mixed up with a shoe salesman who read Blake. He had a great mind, that shoe salesman, really, just great. Some people would have said great in the sense of fat-headed but that was all they knew. Things can be learned from driving rods into the ground, but nowadays they use explosives and that's taken all the fun out of it, all the mystery. She thought the seismograph was a device used by charlatan mind-readers. The last we had heard of her she had eloped with the gimpy alchemist and his retarded assistant, Presumably he changed her.

Once they tried to do fireflies; sat around a meadow one night, friendly at first then silent, then snarling at each other. Oh, the fireflies came all right, but never enough at once and they could never anticipate a blink. After that they pretty well stuck to artificial flowers. Once they went to Stonehenge and came back with the flu. But they could work together and every man Jack of "em had a taste for endive. They hung together . . . just like pirates. *You* know.

Chessmen and the far-off lights; things like that drove her crazy after a while. He knew it was coming, he had seen it from very early on. When she had been gone three months, he went too. The memory of them is sharp but it is only a few pictures and the colour is too bright for truth. It's like a one-eyed man catching a ball: lunge at truth and you get a broken nose. (At least that was what he said, but neither he nor his father much believed in the epigrams they both rolled out so easily. "Epigrams are like doughnuts," the father wrote from Burma. "They got holes in the middle.") Everyone pretended to believe it. They were very understanding; and very loathesome.

So the time passed and passes. One wonders how long it can go on. It's the happiness that goes first, and it matters damn little what goes after that. We pick up daisies and dream of train rides. Hate sneaks in like juice into a grapefruit. One day it leaps out at your eye. Something will snap somewhere. Somehow it will get at them sooner or later, the Great Man, Gladys and the Shadow People. Until then: long noses and petulance.

Raphael Anachronic

HIS RIVALS. "Leonardo," said handsome young Raphaello Santi, "What is Leonardo?"

His mistress Lucia said nothing, for the painter only asked questions of himself, and then only questions for which he already had the answer. Lucia had understood this as soon as she met him. She would probably remain his mistress for at least a month.

She said nothing; she refilled his glass with scotch.

"Leonardo is a scientist with a good pencil sharpener. He has a great future . . . programming computers."

"Yes master."

"Yes master," he parodied.

Raphael saw himself as a great wit. He had been polishing that Leonardo cut for six weeks. Lucia was the fifth mistress to have heard it. Raphael had another for Michelangelo: "A great feeling for form has Buonarotti. A great feeling for sculptural effects. With practice he might become a first-rate cartoonist for the sports pages."

"And what of Botticelli, master?"

"Belt up, you silly twit; I ask the questions around here."

A DAY WITH RAPHAEL. It could not be said of Raphael that he was not a hard worker, no indeed! After nights of wine, song and amorous escapade (of reading himself to sleep with Vasari or Walter Pater), the young master would be demanding coffee and croissants from his mistress at eight sharp. He had an expensive Swiss alarm clock. An hour of primping and he was off to the studio or wherever he happened to be doing a fresco just then for he did a lot of frescoes among other things. He also did 5BX in the mornings for his figure.

He took only fifteen minutes for lunch (hot corned beef on rye, a dill pickle, and beer) and was back at it until sharp four for tea.

Raphael would begin the evening at a bar near work. People gathered to pay court. Raphael would say:

"Dali has a facile touch with a brush. He would do well illustrating medical textbooks."

But Raphael did not love the grovellers; he tired of their agreement, saying:

"Of course, I am a well-rounded Renaissance man. I am great at everything. I only paint for money. Money you need to keep the little ladies happy."

Then he would grab his mistress obscenely and everyone would laugh. Disgusting.

RAPHAEL AT THE MUSEUM. In a museum one afternoon, Raphael exhibited to a Japanese mistress he had at that time that he was a well-rounded Renaissance man. (This was one of his favourite motifs: "After crossing the stony desert of the Dark Ages, Man comes at last to the lush garden of the Renaissance; at the centre of that garden is a flower of celestial loveliness; that flower is me.") He went about with a clipboard and wrote down the generic names of all the fossils.

"Walter Pater calls me a scholar," he said.

The Japanese girl was not at all impressed; she was interested only in social formalities. She was very patient, however.

"Now the Jurassic period was a great age," he declared. He then translated the Latin names of the fossils. He had a most limited knowledge of Latin; he bulled through; he could see nothing wrong in this.

"Yes, and so was the Cretaceous, hmm, hmmm."

RAPHAEL MEETS THE HIPPIES. One night, while strolling with his boringly madonna-like mistress Paola, Raphael came upon some hippies. His own hair was below his shoulders so he did not comment upon the hippies' hair. Instead, he said:

"Hey, you."

"Yes?"

"Do you smoke pot?"

"No," they replied with predictable caution.

"I do," said a girl hippie.

"Wait here, Paola," Raphael whispered. "What I have to say is not for your delicate ears." Then Raphael gave the girl hippie a lecture on virtue, beauty, and truth. The hippies nodded their heads enthusiastically. Raphael concluded:

"Furthermore, if you are to be of any use to the world or yourselves, I would suggest you find an occupation appropriate to your talents and constructive to society . . . Like ditchdigging."

Raphael had a lot of snappy remarks like that one.

RAPHAEL FIGHTS WITH TWO MISTRESSES. Raphael only ever had one Russian mistress. She was a third-generation emigrée, and very high strung. Her name was Galina. One night, in hopes of getting to the opera on time, Galina said:

"Raphael darling, I do so loathe missing the whole first act. Would you hurry with your perfume."

Raphael threw her out at once.

"Asian blood," he said. "Paugh!"

Another time Raphael got himself mixed up with a Scandinavian girl named Sigrid. He had a fight with her and she flattened him. It was not that Raphael was afraid to hit a woman, but that he incautiously hit the wrong one. Raphael dearly wished to brag about his physical prowess.

RAPHAEL FLIES IN AN AEROPLANE. On the invitation of a prestigious gallery, Raphael once agreed to fly to another city for an opening. His mistress, Sophia, came along to soothe him and to handle the excess-baggage bankroll.

"My, what a lovely airport," said Sophia.

This infuriated Raphael. The airport was filthy, the other passengers common, the aeroplane had been invented by da Vinci and would therefore not work.

But the stewardess sweet-talked him and Sophia caressed him and at last he agreed to mount the ramp.

"*The Times,*" he demanded in a stage-English accent. "I want my *Times.*"

Sophia had been briefed on *The Times;* she flourished it. For Raphael considered Englishmen the only true travellers and when travelling endeavoured always to pass for one. He was dressed in tweeds, with a tweed cloth cap and sat sweltering under a massive tweed blanket. But his patent leather pointy-toed shoes gave him away.

"Don't let him worry you," Sophia lied to the stewardess. "He's allergic to aluminum."

"Alu*min*ium," Raphael corrected.

Airborne, he scoffed at the sky, utterly blue above the clouds. "Painted better skies at the age of three. Nature: Bah! Humbug!"

He visited the toilet eight times in the belief that he was defecating directly onto the farmers below. After each flush he would hiss, "Peasants," into the hole.

RAPHAEL A COMMANDO. During the war, Raphael distinguished himself with the commandos. He even got the MC. In his eyes this vindicated the statement he had made to the sergeant-major at the recruiting depot:

"Virtue is the basis of all action. I am the world's greatest painter; this requires the greatest virtue; I will therefore be the world's greatest soldier."

He also explained his greatness in these terms to his many war-time mistresses.

If the truth be known, Raphael did very well for a cream puff.

(If the truth be known, Raphael was not in England at all during the war, for he held an Italian passport and would have been interned for the duration.)

RAPHAEL A FINANCIER. In his studio, along with the paraphernalia of his trade, Raphael kept an old peanut butter jar with a slit in the lid. Into this he put at the end of each day all his pennies.

"How practical you are, Raphael," commented his English mistress, Penelope.

"Of course. An artist is essentially the most practical of types."

She effused upon this subject until Raphael realized she thought he was saving for a rainy day.

"Of course not, you nit. I'm going to corner the market in copper."

Nevertheless, he did not throw her out just then, but a few days later in an argument over central heating.

RAPHAEL WATCHES TELEVISION. The only television programmes Raphael could abide were the spear-and-sandal late shows. He was not impressed by the technology ("A da Vincian trick") and not unreasonably claimed he could paint better pictures with his eyes closed. All sitcoms he found idiotic; features he reviled for they were not about him.

But once the conventions of the medium had been explained to him, Raphael could watch such things as "Hannibal and the Elephant Girl" or "The Sword of Tacitus" with quivering delight.

When the triumphant gladiator had his opponent at his mercy and was looking to Nero for a sign, Raphael would cry: "He deserves an honourable death!" and with a look of respect on his weasly face, Nero would turn his thumb down.

"Bravo! Bravo!"

Raphael thought Nero had taken his advice; that's how naïve he was.

RAPHAEL MEETS ANDREW WYETH. Raphael once condescended to go to Chadd's Ford to visit Andrew Wyeth. They got on because Raphael did most of the talking. So long as he stuck to subjects like the superiority of hand-ground pigments, everything was fine. In the evenings they reminisced:

> RAPHAEL: Things were different in the old days . . .
>
> WYETH: Perhaps you knew my father . . . he died tragically in a train wreck . . .
>
> RAPHAEL: No, it couldn't have been in my time . . . the trains were pretty slow in Urbino back then . . .
>
> (Thinks: what a simpleton!)

After a week, though, the differences came out. In the face of such self-assured technical mastery, Raphael felt compelled to bruit about his own talent and charm. He got onto subject matter: "Magnitude . . . sublimity . . ." he declared.

Wyeth threw him out; besides he had been leaving cigar ashes all over.

HIS ARROGANCE. "Raphael, the entire world acknowledges your genius; why then are you so arrogant?"

This was said by Vera, the most perceptive mistress Raphael ever tolerated.

Raphael stopped his scotch glass halfway to his lips. Vera waited quietly. After a while Raphael said:

"I don't know, Vera."

She wondered if it was just his being Italian; did other Italians brag? It was certainly an accepted cliche. Well, yes, he thought it might be so, but then no Italian had so much to brag about as he. After all . . .

"Perhaps it's the old story about the alienation of the artist . . ."

"Bunk!" exclaimed Raphael. He was *cinquecento;* alienation was nonsense. Artists were greater than anyone else, thus the least alienated; the sergeant-major is never out of step.

Later that afternoon Raphael got a call from the Vatican. Leo X wanted another painting.

"Oh boy, oh boy, oh boy!" cried Raphael. "I'll slap off a new madonna for him tomorrow afternoon and really soak him for it. These popes are filthy rich."

He took Vera right downtown and bought himself a dove-grey Ferrari with four on the floor. Raphael knew what was what.

HIS DEATH. Of course, Raphael claimed mastery of all sports; but being a canny fellow with much of his time taken up with work, women and cocktail parties, people found it difficult to put his boast to the test.

Spectator sports offered Raphael a neat compromise. He went with Sandy to a baseball game and with Francesca to a soccer match. He would criticize the players with impunity. But he said: "I do not see the point of watching sports. Surely this is absurd. Especially for me, for I am better by far than these professional hacks."

Also, he said of the crowds: "Rabble."

An English mistress, Cynthia, got him to play a round of golf with her. But he so praised his own play and so ridiculed hers (she was, in fact, quite good) that she stomped off after the ninth hole.

"A product of inferior breeding," Raphael shrugged.

Raphael continued on his own, much puffed up. No one could now question his eccentric method of scoring which was: he would survey the hole from the tee, estimate his desired play, score same, then tee off. So confident was he that he followed a vicious hook into a swamp. He hacked and splashed at the ball for half an hour saying, "That didn't count . . . that didn't count . . ." and then went home with pneumonia and so died.

He was later reported by at least four golfers to have been seen improving his lie.

RAPHAEL: THE CONSIDERED CRITICAL OPINION. When all was said and done the critics decided this: Raphael was a pretty obnoxious guy, but he sure could paint madonnas.

Smoke

"Happy families are all alike;
every unhappy family is unhappy in its own way."
Anna Karenina

HERE CAME the autumn and the bare trees; afternoons for love and evenings before the fireplace. To be a scholar! The wind crying through the trees and a book, many books, and many years later, wisdom. Walks through the silent forest (build a birdhouse over the winter, study the birds who come in the spring) drawing on a pipe: that would be the life.

"You could make black currant jam and apple butter, pungent aromas on the crisp air, at night we would curl up . . ."

"Oh yes! and a dog! An Irish setter, they look so good when the leaves are turning . . ."

That night, however, Gould and Rachel went to a movie and liked it very much and had to allow as they wouldn't see many movies if they lived in the country.

"And it can get very complicated building birdhouses."

Gould and Rachel both believed truly in Nature; but a bit lazily. As the days of spring grew longer, they would talk of getting pussy willows and finally Rachel would go out and buy them. Summer Saturdays saw them picnicking in their backyard. Both wondered if perhaps they weren't escaping from the World (Gould's father, in a spectacular trial, had been convicted of the murder of his wife), but decided Nature was as real as the World. But would the autumn dream remain a dream?

Gould went to see his father after the trial.

"Why did you do it, Dad? Why?"

His father leaned forward and whispered to him: "Son, when I was a little boy, I pulled the wings off a fly; I've always expected to end my days in jail and my time was getting close. I'm sixty-three, you know."

173

But still handsome and proud despite the prison denims.

"My God!"

He told Rachel when he got home: "It was all a bloody mistake, nothing but a mistake, don't you see!"

The old fellow also told the press about this and they went around trying to get comments from the rest of the family. Only Milton, Gould's Machiavellian younger brother, would comment: "They're all mad," he said. "Heh-heh-heh."

GOULD AND RACHEL sat before their fireplace with Paleologue. Paleologue talked in the random way he had about whales and the River Tay. He had read widely. He knew lives of impresarios and could tell which romantic poets had died of consumption and which of syphilis. Rachel was a dunce with maps, Gould could read them quickly and remember them for future reference, while Paleologue called them tyrannies of the mind and made them seem beautiful. Paleologue walked around things, always around.

("But he can't deal *with* things," Rachel once protested.

("That's of no consequence," replied Gould stiffly. He himself could deal with things, having been trained by his father.

(Milton snickered and went into his back room. He could deal with things better than anyone and his contempt for Gould was as massive as an American car.

("Heh-heh-heh."

(Just what the hell went on in Milton's back room?)

"A mistake," Gould blurted out at last. "It was all a bloody mistake."

"What was?" asked Paleologue, and Gould and Rachel, tumbling over one another, told the story of Ralph and the fly's wings.

"Perhaps it's better this way."

Paleologue was given to musing aloud things which were not entirely clear. He refused to explain himself. He was known to have kept silent about statements which only explained themselves five years later. He was reputed to have made comments which would remain obscure for centuries.

174

"I suppose you won't explain what you mean," said Rachel.

"Hmmm," replied Paleologue.

BEHIND the house lay a formal garden. It was into this garden that Gould's father would come in times of stress. When Gould was born Ralph came here and sat in his lawn chair and gazed at the sculptured shrubs. Quiet beauty. Soothing bonds. He sipped a long cool drink. "Ain't it something," he'd say. After a while he took off his shirt to let the sun get at his chest. It was in this way that he caught pneumonia, for the month was January. The hospital authorities would not let him sleep with his wife. This was the cause of much future trouble.

Little Milton, upon being told of this years later, went to Ralph and drove a sucker stick into his buttock. This was also the cause of much future trouble.

The formal garden is now overgrown.

Milton, some would say, is also overgrown.

Ralph no longer sits in his garden sipping a long cool one. But he still says, "Ain't it something."

RACHEL had a sister named Mildred, about the ugliest girl-child imaginable. Ugly but smart. Mildred's first book was an encyclopaedia; she shortly found it wanting and became soon after the youngest person to receive an adult library card. Smart but snotty. About the time of Ralph's revelation about the fly wings, Mildred was doing research for a bestseller on the Second World War. She had learned from the American commander in the Battle of the Bulge that succinct rejoinder: "Nuts!" This was what she said to the reporters.

But worst of all, Mildred and Milton got on famously.

ABOUT this time, Gould came upon a piece of knotted string. He ran at once with it to Rachel.

"Don't you see, this means Ralph is innocent."

"Wowee! And that means the guilty party is . . ." They were by this time dancing about the room, la-le-la-le, and answered Rachel's

Tolmie

rhetorical question in tones of undisguised glee: "The satanic siblings, M&M Inc.!"

Euclid and Euripedes: the law is not a jolly uncle from whom one extorts an ice cream. Gould and Rachel knew the truth, but as their lawyer explained, the knotted string would not much impress a court. Ralph would likely continue to wear the garb of a concrete cowboy. Oh well!

BUT WHAT had the autumn to do with it? The Irish setter bounded about as the leaves settled. It was all too complicated, really.

"But . . ." said Rachel as she tossed a stick for Blaze.

"Yes . . . well . . ."

"Gould, what a beast you are!"

"It's true what I say . . ." Gould always got surly when reprimanded for some sort of talk error. He felt himself a master of the social graces.

"I mean . . ."

The dog bounded about and the leaves fell. Round about the gnarled tree trunks the silence floated like smoke. The light caught it and it glowed. Soft, so soft, an afternoon to be dreamt by a people, an afternoon floating like smoke through the dreams of young men in love, through the silences of bitter clerks and of their barren wives, through the rocking-chair days of old men poignantly done with the whole business, an afternoon to light the coffins of people who at least once in their lives had reached out their hands and closed them and caught (not really believing they would) contentment: for contentment also is a smoke.

"And that reminds me, you'd better cut some more logs this afternoon or we'll freeze tonight."

"Damn it, so soon?"

They would walk some more, then Gould would go along to the woodshed and cut some logs while Rachel went home to make supper.

While the dog Blaze continued to bound and Rachel and Gould toyed with words, Milton and Mildred lay in wait and Ralph sat in his cell, at peace finally to play cribbage for the rest of his days.

Ralph's cell-mate was named Harry the Hammer. Harry was an habitual smash-and-grab man; he was there for five years. When the five years were up he would be out for a month. That month was the only smear on Ralph's future. His wife had been such a bitch.

"Listen Ralph, I hope you don't mind me asking, fifteen two, but did you really do your old woman?"

(When Harry wasn't playing crib he was reading tough English detective novels.)

"I'll put it this way Harry, twenty for two, did you really break that jewellery-store window?"

"Ralph, you're a hard man. You really know how to hurt a guy. I was carrying home that brick so's to build a bookcase, to improve my mind, turn over a new leaf. I was framed. Twenty-eight."

"Yes, exactly. Thirty-one for two."

"Damn it Ralph, what're you doing with a three?"

It looked like five wonderful years. Except that Gould and Rachel were trying their damnedest to ruin it; Milton and Mildred were about to make a minor error; and somewhere behind it all, musing upon a dead bird, stood the shadowy Paleologue.

Ahh, Paleologue, what role did he play, this retiring poet? It was to him that Gould and Rachel had come after Milton and Mildred had robbed the trust company. The treacherous two had been strapped for research funds. The problem of the perfect crime fascinated them. They concocted their own "soft" explosive and cased the job with telephoto cinecameras. They built up complete files on guard movements, vault specifications and daily cash-on-hand fluctuations. The only mistake they made was in under-dosing the watchman's coffee: he was able to recall for police a dim memory of the event.

Needless to say, the police were still searching for a pair of sneering midgets. The others, though, saw through the newspaper accounts at once.

Paleologue said: "Ah yes, young Milton, remarkable tyke. I once beat him at chess."

"What?"

"Oh yes. He had been up all night on some project or other and so was unable to hypnotize me. Sub-orbital trajectories, I believe . . ."

"So that's how he does it!"

"Yes, sub-orbital trajectories . . ."

Cool windless afternoons on the firing range. Milton and Mildred lounge indolently inside the concrete bunker watching the clock count down. The rocket stands on its launching-pad a hundred yards away; they glance at it now and then through a periscope. While Gould and Rachel meander with Blaze some three miles off (this time Paleologue sitting on a crag observing all with whimsical eye), the twisted Tom Swift and his macabre moll are discussing the possibilities of mass mind control . . .

"No Milt, you fathead, you have to . . ."

The rocket, a mere toy now.

However, the day of the rocket was over. The machine had plunged unseeing and unseen into the lake in front of Gould and Rachel's cottage. In any case, the intended victims had not been at home (had sly Paleologue engineered their absence?) and M&M had realized they must deal less remotely with the situation. Today they lay in wait behind a bushy outcropping near the woodshed. In the crook of Milton's arm rested a most remarkable rifle. It was an air gun and the diabolical missile within the chamber was a dead but still warm woodpecker. Engraved upon the barrel was the sinister entwined M&M trademark (vanity alone allowed this breach of security). They conversed as follows:

"Listen, you dumb bitch, will you stop gnashing your teeth, you're making me nervous."

"Stuff it, he's coming."

It was all very well, this wandering through the hardwood grove kicking leaves and tossing sticks for the dog. But Gould had never been very bright; he did not sense the danger.

A flight of geese honked high overhead. Ah! the cycle of nature, the birth and death of the year, yes, yes, etc.

He hung his jacket inside the shed and brought out the saw.

After setting a log in the trough of the sawhorse he bent to work with the grim determination typical of paper-work people. He hummed and whistled and got drunk on the spice of the sawdust. Of course, his flaccid muscles felt the strain in no time at all. Sawdust got down his boots and the dog grew restless from neglect. Hum, yes, the woodcutter's life is not an easy one, not at all. Long hours and little to show for them. But if you want to live close to nature you must put your back into the muscle struggle of all nature's creatures, yes, yes. It's living in the city that's done this to me, in a little while things will be fine, humm, yes, grunt.

But it was not long before Gould had to pause; it was in the moment he straightened up that a "phht" sounded off to one side and the woodpecker shot past, missing Gould by inches. It disappeared into a bed of moss. Gould said, "Huh?" and looked about.

"You bloody numbskull!"

"Shut up and pass me another woodpecker."

"Never mind another woodpecker, let's get the hell out of here. The dog isn't as dumb as your brother." Mildred was already clambering down the knoll and indeed, Milton saw the dog sniffing the air and staring in his direction. Gould was staring into space.

"Blast."

"Get the lard out."

Milton reluctantly followed his sidekick whose fat calves were already flailing the underbrush toward the brook which would confound the dog's nose.

"Blast."

So Gould was saved by his own flab. But Milton and Mildred had not forgotten; someday they would have another try at the despised elder who stood mumbling in confusion in front of the pile of green wood.

GOULD AND RACHEL went to visit Paleologue. He lived in an old house where all the old things were real. He sat them down in leather chairs arranged around a fireplace in his study; he gave them sherry in old Persian glasses. He giggled.

182

"What is there to giggle about, Paleologue? My father is in the jug for a crime he didn't commit while those two disastrous prodigies are running around loose plotting (gasp!) who knows what deviltries."

"Yes, yes."

And Paleologue gave them a lecture on journeys.

Gould also began to wonder about his mother. She hadn't really been all that bad. She could cook nothing well but custard, had been a terrible housekeeper, and had been stupid. But as Paleologue himself had remarked on several occasions, she was "all heart".

In fact, it had been Rachel's mother Melanie who had been a bitch. "A harpie, by gum," Paleologue had said. He would shake his head after such a remark and smile at the wall.

"Careful, Paleologue, that's my mother you're talking about."

"And Mildred's too."

"Damn it, yes, that's true."

And Rachel would shake her head.

Rachel's mother had ostensibly died of more or less natural causes; but upon discovery of the string, Gould and Rachel had begun to wonder about bitchy old Melanie and her high blood pressure.

"Surely not. Mildred was only seven then and Milton was . . ."

"Eight. That might have meant something with ordinary children, but . . ."

"But. Yes. Listen, though, Gould: what could they have had against Mama? I mean . . ."

"What could they have had against Melanie? Against bitchy old . . ."

"Gould! What a horrible thing to . . ."

A lover's spat? Just one of those things? Or had it been planned by Paleologue? Or by M&M? Or by all three? Ahh!

Paleologue whispered: *"Sic semper tyrannis,"* and poked at the embers.

BUT THE AUTUMN was drawing to a close. As the air grew more nippy, Gould worked harder over the sawhorse, for he did not relish cutting firewood during the snows of February. The dog Blaze had at last given in; he was not going to be played with; there would be no more tossing of the stick. Blaze would wander about on his own business, his self-imposed restriction being only that he stay within earshot of the "zaap-zip" of the sawblade.

"Such a season it's been," Gould had said to Rachel the day before at Paleologue's. They had refused a toddy on the grounds that it was not yet time.

"Time," Paleologue had whispered.

"But if you have a beer . . ."

They had been onto the usual thing, and Paleologue seemed to be trying to say something. He hovered over the point like a vulture over a dying goat. "Yes," Rachel was to point out, "and he never descends until it's dead."

"Now Rachel, don't take him too literally. Old Paleologue, you know, has his . . ."

"Old Ralph," Ralph would be saying just then, "has something nice for you Harry," and would be laying down a twenty-four hand.

"Aww, Ralph, it's going to take me a year to catch up."

"So take a year to catch up. We've got all the time in the world, we're not going anywhere."

Untrue!

"Time," whispered Paleologue.

"What's this going on about time, Paleologue?"

Paleologue smiled and considered and said, "I fancy Milton and Mildred are thinking about time."

Rachel began to fidget. .

"Never mind, Rachel, never mind."

"Now look here, Paleologue . . ."

"It doesn't matter."

"Matter," sighed Paleologue and led them off to the zoo. They had the place all to themselves and over the zoo hung the same silence as in the woods. Paleologue said, "See the rhinorceros." His mispronunciations were always charming.

"So what?" said Rachel and Gould said quietly, "Rhi*noc*eros."

184

It was so frustrating. What did the rhinoceros have to do with the autumn; or with Ralph's plight; or with Milton and Mildred of murderous intent? At last Paleologue looked away from the beast and at his two friends. He smiled at them and his eyes were bright with curiosity and concern.

"It doesn't matter, not really. I'll construct an ending for you.

"Milton and Mildred, in an effort to dispose of the two of you, construct a time machine; they plan to send you back to the Mesozoic age. They plan to attack while you are out skating on your lake tomorrow.

"But I will act at last and so thwart them.

"Ralph will be brought to the scene by secret arrangement with the prison authorities.

"The scene, so:

"The lake, smooth and desolate save for Gould and Rachel swooping about and the faithful hound fumbling happily after. On the crest of a far hill the van, in silhouette, draws up. Three or four figures get out, Ralph and his guards, all in the know, everything unofficial, cupping their smokes against the wind, standing in an artful arrangement. I'll see to that.

"Milton and Mildred have set up their apparatus on a promontory . . . the focus is the centre of a cove where you're sure to go a few times . . . an ambuscade. On some pretext . . . to set up a test object . . . I expect they'll have to go out on the ice, furtive little demons scrambling along ape-wise toward their destinies . . .

"Last strokes of the brush: A low grey sky with a nippy breeze, promise of snow, a lot of grey everywhere . . . I, Paleologue, skulking down through the underbrush . . ."

Gould and Rachel were aghast.

"But . . . but . . .

"We don't understand," mournfully.

Paleologue silenced them with a nonchalant toss of the hand. "What does it matter? If you don't like it, construct your own. Mine's probably no better than the next."

"But Milton and Mildred. What . . ."

185

"Humm . . . yes . . . how does this sound: Uhhhh . . ."

"'Milton, you fathead, you didn't turn off the bloody machine.'

"'I know, but look, isn't this Ralph's formal garden?'

"'(Blank) Ralph's formal garden, look over there.'

"Milton follows her point to the pterodactyl grawking over the gomb tree. 'Does that explain what's happened, you knucklehead?'

"But they are of practical natures and not to be intimidated by a few vapid mesozoic reptiles. They have all their lives to develop the necessary technology with which to build a return time machine.

"'We'll be back.'

"'Damn right.'

"'We'll get them yet.'

"'Yeah.'

"Clenched fists at the sky.

"Just in case they should return to the same spot and the same season (and besides the mesozoic is a warm age), they put aside their snowsuits. And the mittens on the string, they're still kids, we must remember.

"But not, it seems, too young. Mildred, with her first blush of modesty, admits she is pregnant.

"'Knock it off, Mildred, you're too young.'

"'Yeah? Well, tell me again in seven months, wiseguy.'

"'Mildred, we're in a fix.'

"But they'll manage. Hate is stronger even than the bonds of time."

The lecture is over. Gould and Rachel do not understand. They stare at the rhinoceros. There is nothing to understand.

At last Paleologue takes pity on them. "It hasn't really happened, you know. That was just one ending, the rhinorceros ending. Come along."

And he takes them to see the kangaroos and the penguins, the wolves and the peacocks. At last he takes them to see the big cats. One lion, braving the chill, paces about his cage. Gould and Rachel stand and stare for the longest time.

"We still don't understand, Paleologue," they say at last. "You're too obscure."

"It's too bad you think that."

Gould and Rachel go away, back to their house in the forest and their dog Blaze. That night they will sit about before the fire reading and drinking hot toddys. The next day they will go skating should the ice be thick enough.

Paleologue, though, stays at the zoo for a long time this afternoon. He stands before the lion as the day darkens into long night and the snow falls softly about him.

"There's naught to understand," he says and the snow falls silently around.

The smoke of autumn is gone.

Poof.

Born in Mabou, Nova Scotia, Ray Smith has lived in Montreal since 1968, where he teaches English literature at Dawson College. In addition to *Cape Breton is the Thought-Control Centre of Canada*, Smith is the author of five novels, including *Lord Nelson Tavern*, *Century*, *A Night at the Opera* (winner of the QSPELL Hugh MacLennan Prize for Fiction), *The Man Who Loved Jane Austen*, and most recently *The Man Who Hated Emily Bronte*. A new novel, *Mayor Bottomly Among the Virgins*, will be published in spring 2007. (PHOTO: BURT COVIT)